Vorvong and Saurivong
A Cambodian Tale

RECOUNTED BY
AUGUSTE PAVIE

Translated From Pavie's
Original French BY
Marie-Helene Arnauld

Introduction, Editing,
Additional Translation
and BOOK Design by
Joel Montague and Jim Mizerski

Includes All 51
of the Original Illustrations

PUBLISHED BY DATASIA PRESS
2019
www.DatAsia.us

"To Cambodia's kings, its chiefs, its priests, and its people"
(*Mission Pavie Indo-Chine, 1879 - 1893,*
Etudes Diverses, I, pages XI-XII)

© Copyright Original Translation, Text and Design, 2018:
Marie-Hélène Arnauld, Joel Montague, and Jim Mizerski

ISBN: 978-1-934431-22-1

TABLE OF CONTENTS

Auguste Pavie (center, back) as he dressed on his missions
ca 1893, Wikimedia Commons

INTRODUCTION

Beginning in 1869, August Pavie (1847-1925) served as an enlisted Marine infantryman, civil servant, explorer and diplomat for France in Indochina, Cambodia, Laos and Siam. He retired to France in 1904.

As one of the greatest explorers of Southeast Asia, Pavie devoted the years between 1879 and 1895 to exploring Cambodia, Siam and Laos. He then documented his work in a collection of eleven books broadly entitled *Mission Pavie Indo-Chine* published in French between 1898 and 1919.

It may come as a surprise to most readers that the first volume[1] of *Mission Pavie*, the source of the tale translated in this text, has little to do with geography, politics or exploration but is a collection of five folk tales. Three of those tales were also printed in Khmer text, and two of those were also printed in Laotien and Siamese texts. The Khmer text for "Vorvong and Saurivong" appears to be a careful copy of a rare palm-leaf manuscript.

In 1881 on his way from Kampong Som to Oudong in Cambodia, Pavie was stranded with his interpreter by a heavy rain one night at a roadside sala[2] for travellers. When the rain stopped, Kol, his interpreter, went to ask for some food at a nearby village. The villagers brought platters of food as well as mats and pillows. The villagers wondered if Pavie would like to come to hear Uncle Nop, who was visiting their village from a neighboring hamlet to read the story of "Vorvong and Saurivong." Pavie agreed.

He was truly impressed by Uncle Nop's reading, his moving performance of the story and the villagers enthusiastic reception. Describing what happened next, Pavie wrote[3]:

---

1 *Mission Pavie Indo-Chine, 1879 - 1893*
Etudes Diverses, I, Recherches sur la Litterature du Cambodge, du Laos et du Siam par Auguste Pavie.
Paris, Ernest Leroux, Editeur, 19 Rue Bonaparte, 1898

2 A small roadside pavillion to shelter travellers

3 Mission Pavie, Etudes Diverses, vol. 1, XLI

> He finished reading the whole story. Thanking him, I asked him to entrust me with the old palm-leaf manuscript he had read to us.
>
> "Simply," I said, "just the time to make a copy. I have a keen desire to have in my hands such a charming work, to reproduce it, if I may later, by our easy printing process, and to spread many copies throughout your villages."
>
> He handed it to me, recommending it as a treasure dear to him and to the people of the country.
>
> All with the old man read in my eyes, better than my words did not know how to say, how much I appreciated this mark of trust and my great desire to lead one day to the end I wished and the wish born in them.
>
> Today, seventeen years having passed, what a joy I feel for the accomplishment!
>
> "Oh dear Khmer country, as I look back at all this past!"

The translation of "Vorvong and Saurivong" was made in pieces during Pavie's leisure time, from 1889 to 1894, with the successive assistance of four Cambodian collaborators: Mr. Oum,who did most of the work, Mr. Takial, Mr. Tchioum and Mr. Chiaup. Pavie said that, as it is was a popular story, it was not intended to be a word for word translation.

Pavie wrote that:

> According to Buddhist usage, the authors show in the hero of the drama the personification of the last Buddha in various of his many incarnations. It is therefore useless to say how great is the place in which their stories hold the supernatural. [1]

The original illustrations used for Pavie's 1898 book were copied from the frescos adorning the walls of the pagodas of the region. Although the source illustrations were all in color, only twenty were reproduced in color in Pavie's book since they had to be printed separately and individually inserted into the books at their proper locations, an expensive process..

---

1 Ibid, XI

In 1902 Pavie published another short (15 pages) Cambodian tale, "Mea Yeung," in La Revue (Ancienne Revue des Revues) that included 18 small illustrations.

In 1903 Pavie published another short book of five abbreviated folk tales entitled Contes Populaires du Cambodge, du Laos et du Siam that contained no illustrations.

Then in 1921 he published Contes du Cambodge that contained the 1898 book tales along with the twenty color illustrations but none of the 31 monochrome illustrations from "Vorvong and Saurivong. It also included the 1902 tale of "Mea Yeung." The preface to the 1921 publication revealed that an all-Khmer book with the copy of Uncle Nop's palm-leaf manuscript was published in an edition of 500 copies that were distributed to the pagodas of Cambodia.

Finally, in 1921 Pavie published Sanselkey, a short (56 pages) Cambodian tale extracted from Contes du Cambodge but with 5 previously unpublished drawings by a Cambodian artist and a number of "bandeaux et culs de lampe" (see page ii).

In Mission Pavie, Pavie wrote that publishing the folk tales in 1898 in Cambodian script as well as in French was as a testament to show his gratitude to Cambodia's kings, its chiefs, its priests, and its people for the invaluable help they provided and the countless services rendered during his journey, and to show their extremely interesting populations in a more accurate light.1

It is in the same spirit that this first English language translation of Auguste Pavie's "Vorvong and Saurivong," with all of its delightful orginal illustrations, is published.

---

1 Ibid, XI-XII

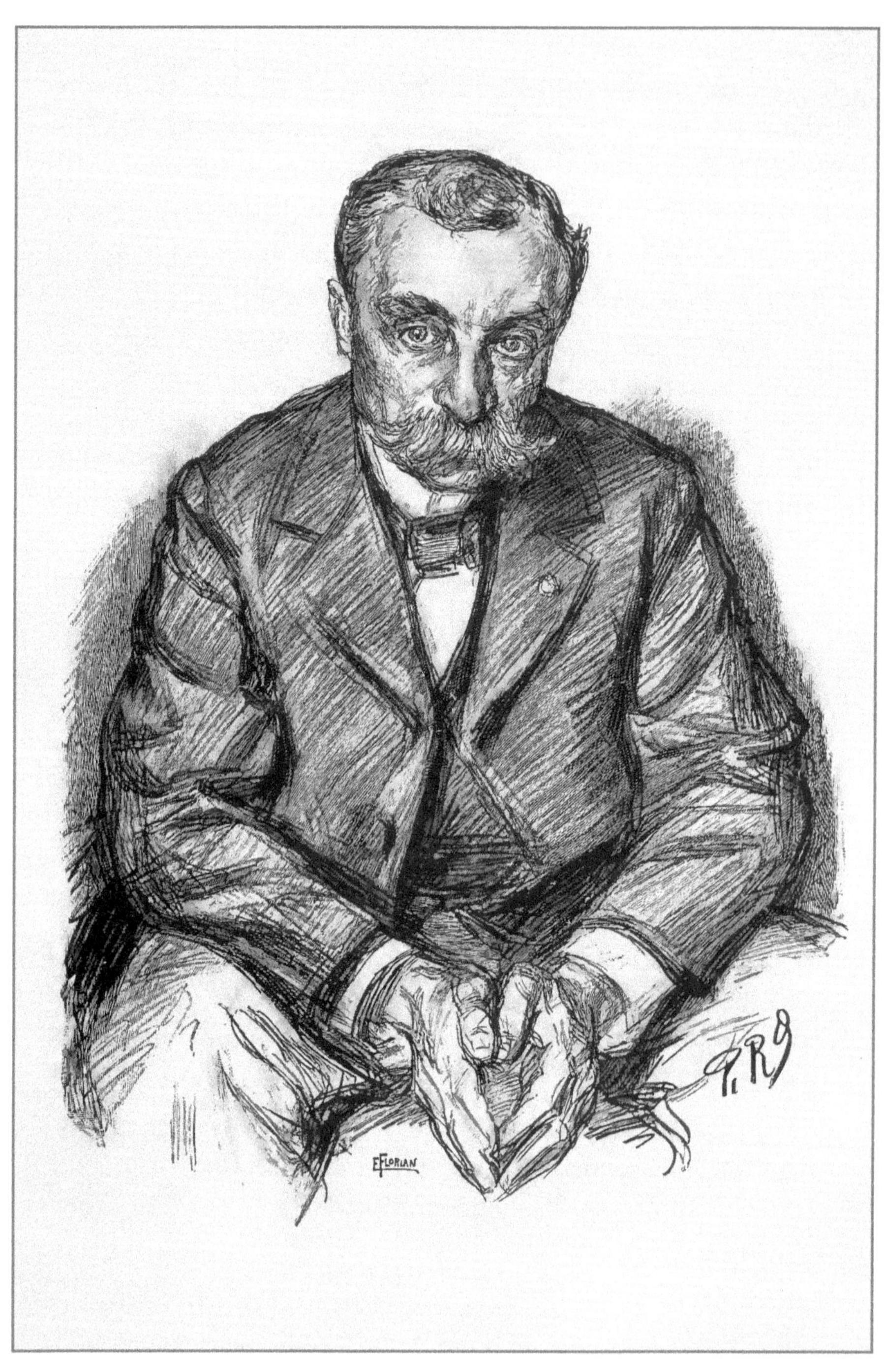

Auguste Pavie, ca 1901
(*Mission Pavie Indochine, 1879-1895, Geographie et Voyages, I*)

VORVONG AND SAURIVONG
A CAMBODIAN TALE

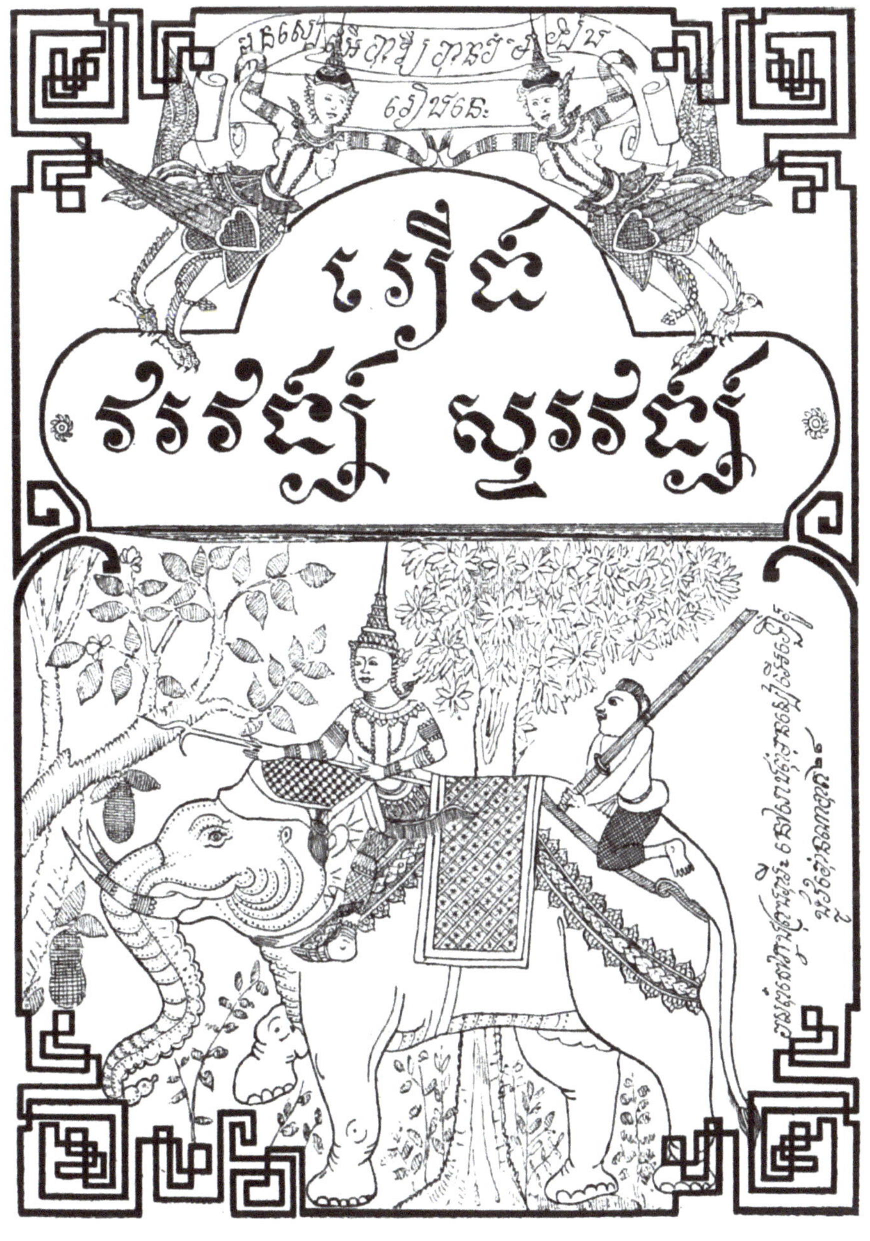

Figure 1

CHAPTER I - TREACHERY AND EXILE

Once upon a time there was a king named Sauriyo; his country was the Kingdom of Creassane. **(Figure 1)**

The Queen, his wife, was so beautiful that she could be compared with the celestial angels. Her name was Tieya.

One night, she had an extraordinary dream. An anchorite holding a crystal ball all aglow with various lights came down from the sky toward her, saying: "Unique princess, take this jewel; it allows the person who holds it in their hand to fly and is worth more than a kingdom. You will keep it by being devout and should you want a second one, your wish will be fulfilled."

Almost immediately, he placed another ball in the Queen's hand and ascending into space he added: "This one is even more precious than the first one."

Neang[1] Tieya, so happy to receive those two marvels, raised them above her head.

In the morning when she woke up, she told the King about her dream. Full of joy, the King concluded that they would have two children and one of them would have qualities beyond what one could ever imagine.

Soon afterwards, the Queen became pregnant. Surrounded by her husband's attentions, she gave birth to her first son after ten months[2].

The following year, also after ten months, a second boy was born. From his features, the soothsayers recognised that in terms of wisdom, he was as wise as a priest.

When the princes had grown up, the King called them Sauvirong and Vorvong. He loved them very much. The chiefs and

---

1 Neang is a women's name.

2 It is an old Cambodian belief that a child is better suited for a long time in the womb of his mother.

the people were also very fond of them.

The King had a second wife, Neang Montea. She happened, after ten months, to give birth to a boy, Vey Vongsa.

The King loved that child as much as the previous two. He enjoyed providing his three sons with all kinds of toys for their entertainment.

Vey Vongsa was now five.

Neang Montea had a detestable heart, she could not stand having someone above her. The idea that the Queen had two children who, when they were grown up, would occupy the throne, drove her mad.

She thought that in case of rebellion, both of them would stand with each other. "While one was in battle", she thought, "the other would be building fortresses." Her single child would never be able to fight against them. This nasty woman was constantly looking for means to make Sauvirong and Vorvong perish.

One day the two brothers were wandering around the palace; the elder was seven and the younger was six. They went within sight of Neang Montea. She was glad to come across them; she wanted to ensure their loss straightaway.

"Come, my dear children, I am happy to see you, let me kiss you." Hearing those kind words from their second mother, both came near her respectfully. She kissed them, caressed them, then all of a sudden, she pressed them between her knees and called for help.

> Please set me free from these young boys who have united to assault their father's wife!
>
> Oh, King Sauriyo, you who loved me before, why do you hate me now and make me so unhappy! Why let your children throw themselves onto me like this and batter me? If you have no feelings for me anymore, expel me but don't let me be dishonored like this!

Her calls brought everybody together; the King came down from his throne. He saw his sons and Neang Montea and out of anger, he beat his own body and cried: "How can small children commit such an abomination? Surely, when they are older they will rebel against me. I cannot let them live!"

And as his fury increased, he forgot that they were his children and he called the executioners. He ordered them to capture them, tie them up, take them far away, behead them and then bury them immediately.

The executioners received the order from the King and went and seized the two brothers. **(Figure 2)**

One feels very sorry for the little princes for the horrible fate which Neang Montea subjected them to!

In tears they called to their mother: "Dearest mother, have mercy on us; we are so young; we did nothing wrong. Why is our father sentencing us? Go and beg his mercy, oh dear mother!"

At the beginning, the executioners did not dare to be rough with the little princes; however, realising that they had been ordered by the King, they tied them up and took them toward an isolated wood. **(Figure 3)**

On hearing her sons' calls the queen fainted; but soon she got up and then ran after them towards the forest. She caught up with them and fell to the ground crying. Then she went towards them and embraced them still in tears.

> Dear children, you are captives; a fatal pain is in my heart! Since your birth, you did not leave me, and you never suffered the heat from the sun! When putting you to bed every evening, your mother never feared anything for you. She held you tight in her arms!
>
> And now, a tragedy has arrived; someone wants to kill you both and bury you. Oh, my darlings!
>
> As soon as she saw that you were condemned, your

Figure 2

Figure 3.

Figure 4

mother came to join you; my dear children, my heart is broken! When I used to see you every day, sorrows seemed less painful. Now I think that my heart is broken! If they kill you, I want to die. Why should I remain on earth after my children's death? My little ones are the sons of a king and one shows great consideration for their glorious births!

Her face was drenched with tears. "Why didn't you die when you were inside me? I couldn't stay behind and live; now I want to die!"

Her body was shaking and tears were continuously running down from her eyes. She beat her chest and blackened it with her blows. Her throat was dry and soon she collapsed on the ground, exhausted and stiff.

The two darlings started to weep.

Saurivong said:

> Mother, you who love us so much and came here to find us, why, when we saw one another again, did you die? We don't know what to do, dear mother, you who fed us; if you are not going to get up and answer us, we will die next to you!
>
> Dear brother, let us pray; let us ask that life be returned to our mother. **(Figure 4)**
>
> Oh spirits, you who live in the ten directions, and all of you angels of the sky, the two of us, very faithful to our parents, we beg you to come and make our mother come back to life. Our good lords, answer our prayer!

Little Vorvong, still crying, holding his mother tightly with both hands also said:

> Oh, beloved mother, for the love of us, you followed us all the way here. Your face is as red as blood. You cared so much for us and were pained so much by our misfortune that after having cried all the tears in your eyes, you fainted and succumbed. Oh, dearest mother, the favors you bestowed on us were bigger than the earth and the sea together. Your caring was so sweet to us! Now we are going to perish in the middle of this lonely forest, so we are saying our last prayers to the angels.

> Oh, angels, you who occupy the surrounding ravines, valleys and mountains, please rescue our dear mother. Listen to me, oh you who live in the regions of the sky; listen to our last prayers!
>
> Both of us have always been faithful to our dear mother. Have compassion for the woman who gave us life, help her, bring her back to life as she was in the past!

Thanks to the kindness of Heaven, life immediately was returned to the Queen and she woke up following her children's wishes.

Straightaway she embraced her two beloved sons. "My darlings, had I fallen asleep?"

They both replied: "You were not sleeping; you had lost your life. We begged the angels to return it to you, and it is thanks to them that you are able to hold us tightly like this."

Realising what they were saying, she then said: "It is better to die rather than to endure separation. I can only be happy if you are alive next to me."

The executioners witnessed the death of the Queen, they heard the little princes' prayer and they saw the angels answer it. They were surprised and, nodding, they looked at one another; they didn't wish to deprive them of their lives anymore. They knelt down, bowed and said:

> Dear Queen, we recognise the power of your glorious children. The King ordered us to behead them; we couldn't do it. We are going to let them escape, then we will tell the King that both of them were killed and their corpses were burned.
>
> Do not be alarmed by us; we will keep the secret; but, dear masters, vanish straightaway. Escape to foreign countries.

Hearing them, the Queen was overjoyed, the weight of her pain was reduced and she felt happy. To the executioners she said:

Dear executioners, my children are still alive now and you are the persons who brought it about. This good deed is incomparable! You are the sea shore for shipwrecked victims! As long as I live, you will never be short of anything. I will shower you with gifts and your wishes will be fulfilled.

Overjoyed, the Queen, fearless, immediately returned to her palace. She prepared two shoulder bags, filled them with food and then took two remarkably crafted rings adorned with diamonds and, going back to her little ones, she gave the gifts to them and said:

My dear children, I possess no other fortune than these two rings; they are yours. The stones that they are adorned with are worth a kingdom. When you break your journey, should you lack some light or fire, hold them; their sparkle is equal to that of a flame. Gather some twigs and dried leaves; their contact with the diamonds will light them and then all you will have to do is place the branch of a tree on top of them in order to cook your food.

My beloved sons, when you walk through the forests and the valleys, watch out for ferocious animals and buffaloes.

You are going to wander aimlessly, but you will be under the protection of Heaven, and your mother is certain of this: you will come back in ten years' time from now. In the meantime, suffering from sadness, she will, in vain, desire death.

The Queen, joining all her courage to her love, held them tightly in her arms. The two children said farewell to her and left. Then invoking the spirits who inhabit the springs, the forests and the neighboring mountains, Neang Tieya asked them to watch over her sons.

The executioners told the King: "We killed your children; their bodies have already been burned."

Hearing their words, he was satisfied and replied: "Burning them was not necessary; burying them in the forest would have been enough. Who can blame us for what happened because of them?"

Hearing that the queen could not stop weeping, he got angry with her and insulted her, saying: "You, heartless and silly woman, whose children have so severely offended me, why are you shedding tears like this? Do not remain in my palace. Get out or I will have you carried out by the guards."

When Neang Tieya heard those words, she was frightened and dared not to utter a word. She went out without being assisted by anyone, weeping over her misfortune. The King, in his rage, abandoned her totally. Later he did not enquire about her, and she never tried to see him.

CHAPTER II - ROYAL DESTINIES

The young princes had gone alone far away.

Both of them, overwhelmed with distress and walking in the lonely woods, were thinking about their mother all the time, even forgetting how unhappy they themselves were. They reached the large country of Baskim, the King of which was Kietat Meanok.

By a special favor of Heaven they had covered more than sixty leagues in a single day.

There, there was a big market; precious objects were surrounded by numerous buyers from many countries. Seeing the two children, they looked at them, astonished, and murmured: "They are so beautiful!"

The shop keepers talked among themselves, stating: "They are so much alike and so sweet; if they were given to us to be our children, we would accept them with pleasure."

Some of them, after having chatted, asked:

> Where have you come from, poor children, all on your own? Did you lose your way far from your mother? Tell us, we would like to help you.
>
> Why aren't you answering?
>
> You don't seem to be hearing anything and are walking along the market, silent.

They held them tightly in their arms, gave them cakes and covered them with their scarfs. **(Figure 5)**

Touched by the kindness of the people of Baskim, they walked with tears in their eyes and thought: "Let us not feel sorry for ourselves, let us only think about our mother who, no doubt, is crying and choking with grief."

Leaving the region, they entered a superb forest full of water springs and ponds, crisscrossed by numerous streams as well as a pretty river flowing smoothly. Beyond the forest they

Figure 5

reached the mountains surrounded by a meadow of a beautiful light green color in which all sorts of animals were grazing. Not being able to find a path, the two princes, exhausted with fatigue, sat down in the shade of a large fig tree.

Poor little princes, you had been so happy! Separated from your mother, far away from your country, you now cruelly suffer the punishment of the offences committed in a previous life!

Looking at the mountains, in their quiet solitude, they saw the wonderful scene of blooming vegetation at the very moment when the sun, losing its light, hid behind the high mountains.

Then, looking for a shelter, they climbed up a tree and tied themselves to a branch for the night; but they couldn't sleep. Sadness showed on their faces, they were heavy hearted and their eyes were full of tears.

They kept saying: "We are so unhappy; our fate is beyond compare. Are we dead or alive? When she left us, our dear mother said:

> Children, your mother is saying goodbye but she promises you will return in ten years' time. If on that date you have not come back, she will die, unable to stand her pain any longer. Now you are going to wander and spend the nights in solitude in the forests inhabited by ferocious animals which will threaten your life. The thought that she could die without seeing you again will constantly be torturing her."

Then they said: "May heaven protect us and let us live like other humans so that we can come back and make her happy."

They could hear the night birds and the roaring of wild animals. It was midnight when at last they fell asleep. Through a special favor, the awareness of what happened reached heaven. Pra En[1] the powerful, felt a blast of hot air like what might be produced by the burning of a divine temple

Guessing that something unusual was taking place, Pra En

1 Indra

with his sharp eyes scanned the earth and noticed the two children on the branch of a tree. They were locked in an embrace and sound asleep. He understood the cause of their presence there. Grabbing the Book of Existence, he realised that being born from Buddha they were, after many changes, close to reaching Nirpean[1]. "I must go to their rescue and return a favorable destiny to them," he thought. Pra En called a celestial spirit, Pra Pusnoka.

"Go down to earth, help these two children so that they can be elevated according to their rank and their passing through life marked by their superior deeds."

Hearing those words, Pra Pusnoka, filled with joy, bowed, travelled quickly through space, arrived near the mountain and saw the two children sleeping. He transformed himself into two roosters. One, black, immediately crowed loudly under the tree; the other, white, came down from the mountain, perched itself on top of the branches and screamed with all its strength.

The black rooster, mocking, hailed the white one: "Lord, who do you think you are? Where do you come from and dare to perch on this fig tree? Even I, being among the strongest, wouldn't dare to go so high!"

It went on provoking the other bird:

> Your parents did not bring you up properly since you dare to fight with me over my royal dwelling place. Remember this, whoever will eat my flesh, will, seven years later, be king of two kingdoms. Your screams, the noise of your wings up there, are offending me; come down and show your strength and your courage!

The white rooster replied:

> You are no doubt of low birth to be living like this under the tree. Being powerful and strong, I reside on the top of the mountains. You had better remember this: Whoever will eat my flesh will, seven months later, reign over two king-

1 Nirpean, Nirvana, Paradise

doms for the rest of their life. You want to fight? Alright, try and hold out against me!

Pra Pusnoka, by transforming itself in this way, wished to let the two princes be unaware that heaven came to their rescue. Woken up by the noise and understanding that the roosters were going to fight, Vorvong said to his brother: “Choose one of these roosters!” **(Figure 6)**

Saurivong answered: “Take the black one or the white one, as you wish; later we will see which one is the winner.”

But Vorvong bowed and said: “I am the younger; I must take the black rooster; it is of course, very inferior to the white one.”

Saurivong said: “It doesn’t matter; take the one you want.”

At that very moment, the white rooster jumped down from the top of the tree and a fierce fight began. At dawn both roosters succumbed.

The children watched and followed their fight; but seeing them dead, they rushed towards them and Vorvong took the black one and Sauvirong the white one. They plucked them, cooked them and assuaged their hunger. They saved what was left and got going again.

Seven months went by without them meeting anybody. The memory of their mother was still present in their minds.

One evening, in the Kingdom of Conthop Borey, they found themselves in front of an inn put at the disposal of travelers. Everything there was quiet. They went in, lied down and fell asleep.

It was the country of King Visot. Surrounded by a large army, loved by his numerous people and his chiefs, King Visot had governed until a very old age but he had been dead for seven months. With his wife, Queen Komol Melea, he had left behind a single daughter, perfect in beauty and virtue,

Figure 6

adored by her parents and cherished by everyone. To her natural charms, Princess Sar Bopha added a rare intelligence; she loved books and enjoyed the most complicated mind games. The dignitaries, the Brahmans and the scholars were in pursuit of the pleasure of seeing her and listening to her. She put to them bright questions and enigmas, answered theirs cleverly and often they had to bow before her amazing subtlety.

However, the most important people in the country had in vain held several councils for the choice of a successor to the throne. Seeing the people in tears looking for support, they resorted to the calculations of the astrologists and delivered this suggestion to the queen:

> Dear Queen, the person we need to lead the people properly and be our glorious sovereign is in the Kingdom. We beg you, have the sacred elephant decked out and let it go as it pleases. It will go straight to the predestined person to whom the divine gift of our country will have been offered by heaven. It will kneel in front of that person, will greet him, snatch him respectfully, place him on the royal cushion and bring him to the capital.

They had hardly finished when the Queen gave the orders.

The elephant, seemingly happy about its mission, left, proudly bowing, and went towards the north.

In the isolated inn in the middle of the forest, the young princes were fast asleep following their long fatigue and hardships. They didn't wake up when suddenly the royal elephant followed by a long retinue triumphantly stopped its course there, very close to them.

The intelligent animal nodded, knelt down and bent down on its four legs, down to their level. It gently put its delicate trunk around Saurivong's body, the elder boy. Without interrupting his sleep, it carefully put him in place and quickly returned to the palace, as the scholars had stated. **(Figure 7)**

As he was woken up by the procession leaving, Vorvong

Figure 7

was so surprised and frightened when he couldn't see his brother next to him, but saw the crowd of chiefs and soldiers close to the house. He ran away and he got lost in the depth of the woods. The noises which the wind was carrying increased his fright so he hid inside the hole of a tree.

Having been carried away by the elephant, Saurivong woke up in the palace surrounded by officers and servants anxious to please him. When he did not see his brother whom he first thought had been taken with him, he worried and he shed some tears and asked: "My good lords, can you tell me where my beloved brother is? We were sleeping next to each other. Why did you take me without him? I beg you, bring him back to me!"

They all bowed: "We did not know you had a brother, glorious prince, the elephant which has just come back brought you alone."

Given his despair, they left and went to the forest thinking that they were going to find Vorvong there. When they returned, they could only say: "The house in which the elephant took you is empty; our searching was useless."

And so, Saurivong gave way to his sorrow.

When at last reason calmed him down a little, and when he saw that he, who was only a child, was introduced to warriors, servants and all the people who were retinue of kings, he asked: "Why did you take me; what do you want from me?"

All the dignitaries replied:

> We now know that you were two young princes who had left their family in search of a knowledgeable hermit able to educate them. We, the chiefs of this old country whose king is no more, and since we do not have among us a man suited to the supreme power, we wish to have you as sovereign and master in this palace where a happy destiny is bringing you.
>
> Our gracious Princess Sar Bopha, the only daughter of our King, will become your wife and our Queen.

Figure 8

Saurivong found this offer, coming from the dignitaries of the Kingdom of Conthop Borey who had bowed down in front of him, difficult to refuse; so, he accepted it.

Queen Melea was immediately informed of the arrival of the prince recommended by Heaven. She ordered that his elevation as well as that of Princess Sar Bopha be quickly arranged.

Let us now leave Saurivong in the middle of the big ceremonies and let us go back to Vorvong. **(Figure 8)**

When the setting sun colored the tall trees crimson, Vorvong in his hideout, desperate, bemoaned the loss of his brother:

> Maybe he is dead; if so life would be unbearable for me; I could not return to my father's kingdom without him! Taken away from our mother's affection, both of us united, we could bear our fate; but we cannot be apart forever! Who will be able to help me to find my brother!

Searching and calling for Saurivong, he remembered the house where he lost him; his tears were running down in abundance. Walking barefoot on the dry ground, devoid of trees or lawn, he moved away along the path, turning around all the time and recalling the long months of their journey through the forests inhabited only by ferocious animals.

He then found himself at the gate of the city where, without his realising it, his brother was in despair just like him. He went to the guards and asked: "You who never leave your post, have you seen my brother going in?"

Those rude men, unhappy about having been disturbed, nastily said: "Who is this child who dares to disturb the King's guards? If his brother had come this way, who could have recognised him since they had never seen him before? Make sure, vermin, that you don't come back at night and trouble our sleep." To those nasty words, they added some insults and threatening gestures.

Little Vorvong left the premises fearfully and took a path at random. After seven days during which he often prayed for the spirits to protect him from the ferocious animals, he found himself in the kingdom of Pohoul Borey. The capital was surrounded by walls; the palace with gleaming multicolored roofs, gold, green, red, blue was that of King Thornit whose favorite wife, Queen Kramoth, died leaving behind her a daughter.

Neang Kessey was the most pleasant and accomplished among all the princesses. Her supernatural beauty and the incomparable harmony of her slim body, were not unlike that of celestial angels. To a most rare intelligence she had added, despite her young age, the most varied knowledge.

Raised by her father, who was jealous of her treasure, she lived in sumptuous solitude surrounded by ladies of the court and carefully selected servants.

Near the palace an old woman was cultivating flowers, bouquets of which she would bring to her every morning and evening. Night had come, thunder was roaring and the sky which had darkened with clouds suddenly released some torrential rain.

Vorvong, who was forced to stop, looked for a shelter in the light of the lightening. He spotted the old lady's hut. He went close to it and, standing at the door, he called: "Oh, obliging friend, allow me to come into your home during the downpour!"

The old woman asked: "Where have you come from in the middle of the night?"

"From a faraway country. I have been separated from my brother on the way. I am shivering in the rain; have pity on me!"

"I am a poor flower lady, my garden hardly provides me enough to live on; my house is so small, I haven't got much room to cook my food even. If you came in, we would not be able to move; however, since you are cold, take shelter."

Poor Vorvong climbed up a ladder and sat in a corner, chilled to the bone. Hunger was torturing his stomach. He couldn't stand it, so he asked: "Wouldn't you have a little rice, some left over from your meal? Please, spare it."

"How can you be so audacious! Where do you come from? I gave you shelter; isn't that enough? Do I also have to feed you?"

> Dear old lady, for seven months I have been wandering all over, enduring the toughest hardship. I have been continuously walking, feeding on fruit from the trees. I have forgotten the taste of rice; exhausted due to my suffering I dare to tell you that I am hungry. Give me some relief, please!

"If this is the case then, have a look in the pot close to the wall and you will find the leftovers from my meal there."

Filled with gratitude, Vorvong thanked her, got up and went into the kitchen. The darkness forced him to ask for a light.

But the old woman, agitated to be once more disturbed, spoke some more harsh words: "Now you need a torch; I don't have any; you are too demanding and impudent. I gave you a shelter and some food; now stop disturbing my sleep."

Then he thought about his ring. He thought: "The ring my mother gave me has the most precious stone."

"For want of light", his mother had said to him, "all you have to do is put it on your finger, it will shine, and with it you can also cook food very quickly." He slid the ring on his finger and a bright beam emerged.

The lady thought her torch was shining and she became angry. "The remainder of the torch which I was saving so carefully, he is burning it unnecessarily!"

She got hold of a stick and ran to the kitchen, saying: "I am going to teach him a proper lesson."

Seeing that the light was coming out of Vorvong's ring, she stopped, confused, and she then mistook him for a thief. She ran towards the palace and arrived in front of the sovereign.

"Supreme Master, a thief has taken refuge in my house. On his finger is shining a beautiful ring with extraordinary lights; it can only belong to the Royal Treasury."

Hearing these words, the King commanded the guards: "Follow this woman, arrest the thief. Put a cangue around his neck, chains around his ankles and make sure that he cannot escape."

The guards arrived in front of the hut and the old lady murmured to them: "He is in there; be careful and grab him quickly. Take him to the King and punish him the way he deserves."

Realising that he was all of a sudden surrounded and chained, the poor boy, shaking and crying, begged the angels in heaven to come to his rescue. (**Figure 9**)

Without wanting to hear anything, the guards took him away. The King did not have him either questioned or tried; he was locked up in a cage with the cangue still around his neck and chains around his ankles and he was not allowed any food.

Feeling so unhappy, Vorvong foresaw death approaching. The memory of his mother and her kind care then came and filled his mind. He thought about the recognition that he owed her; her dear image always present in his eyes gave him some courage and helped him bear his cruel fate. He understood that the pain he was enduring erased the mistakes of a past life.

For six years he remained without eating anything; he shed so many tears that at last he inspired some pity.

Royal astrologists looked into the stars for the cause of the suffering endured by such a young child. One of them explained that the suffering represented the punishment for having been guilty in the past:

Figure 9

In a previous existence, this child, an avid animal hunter, killed a large number in the ravines and mountains. One day, caught up in a storm, he took shelter in an abandoned hermitage. A beautiful pair of stags, scared by the rumbles of thunder, sheltered there at the same time as him. Filled with joy, the young boy grabbed the male by its hairy horns and tied it up thinking that by doing so he could keep the doe near him; but it ran away. He went after it and couldn't catch it so he came back to the stag, took it away and kept it captive in a cage. It is this crime which the prisoner is paying for.

The scholars also asked:

Since he has been deprived of food for such a long time, he has become as thin as a leaf. How is it that he did not die of hunger? It would have happened to any other human being!

A black rooster, the flesh of which he ate, was no other creature than a metamorphosed Pra Pusnoka; ten thousand years of extra hardship would not take his life.

His glorious origins, the merits he acquired by coping with his pain and above all the admission that in his thoughts he did not stop talking to his mother, at last attracted Pra-En's attention.

The powerful Sovereign of Heaven was suddenly obsessed with the idea that a deed showing his kindness had become urgent on earth. Leaving his divine residence, the Supreme Intelligence saw that the child in the cage was born into the race of the Buddha. He questioned the Book of Existence, realised that the pain he was enduring would soon come to an end, and that the review of his past lives should give him an easier freedom. "Charming Kessey", he thought, "does not realize that her fiancée is not far from her. Let us go and inform her and put an end to our dear child's miseries."

In the dead of night, he crossed through space and came to the palace where the young girl was sleeping. (**Figure 10**)

In a dream, she saw him, he talked to her and she heard

Figure 10

him: "The future partner in your life, a prince born into the race of Buddha, is enduring a difficult misfortune close to you. Generous princess, are you going to remain indifferent to his sorrow any longer?"

Neang Kessey woke up, sat up on her bed and tried to remember her dream:

> A Brahman saint talked to me; then he vanished! I haven't forgotten his words. The young foreigner who has been captive for six years in the cage is the only one whom I have heard tell his misfortune.
>
> The thought that it is him is already moving me. Shouldn't I go to the poor prisoner straightaway and find out who he is and what I have to do?

Confused, she knelt down and sent an ardent prayer towards the heavens asking for inspiration and light. Then she felt determined.

She relied on the benevolent Pra En and, entrusting him with her being, put on her clothes, came down from her residence and walked into the dark night. In the apartments, the servants were sleeping and all the guards at the gate had fallen asleep.

The eyes of the prisoner were roving sadly in the dark; suddenly they were staring. A young girl was approaching. Her supernatural beauty and the harmony of her svelte body reminded him of the celestial angels. Just like a divine vision, she was walking towards the cage. This incomparable creature, Vorvong had never seen her pass by. He felt he was the victim of an illusion, a dream, and he worried about it vanishing.

Then he thought she was probably a messenger from the heavens, able to put an end to his horrible misery. He tried to please that messenger by saying: "Kind spirit, you who are coming alone in the darkness of the night, why do you seem to be hesitating? Hear my prayer. Allow me to talk to you; tell me who you are!"

She was all smiles and, in her soft voice, she said:

> I am the King's daughter! In my sleep, a short time ago, a messenger from heaven appeared and told me: 'Your future life companion, a prince born from the race of Buddha, is enduring a harsh misfortune, not far from you. Generous Kessey, will you remain indifferent to his sorrow longer?'
>
> Through my prayer, I entrusted the angels with my destiny, thinking that you were indeed the prince of my dream, I left my room and the palace, trustful, and came to you. On my way out, I saw the servants and the guards fast asleep, which was a sign that heaven was protecting my moves. Tell me about your family, your country, your story. I would be very happy if from your own voice I heard confirmation of the hope which began in my heart.

The prince, moved with joy, understood that this delightful young girl had been his companion in previous lives and that she was becoming his fiancée. He said: "Dearest sister, your dream having come true has brought us together again, I feel my relief is near; the night, thanks to the goodness of the angels, will allow me to relate my sorrow."

She sat down, attentive and at a slight distance, and so the captive began: **(Figure 11)**

> My country is the Kingdom of Creassane.
>
> King Sauriyo's capital contains a lot of palaces; his army is innumerable; he possesses one hundred territories he can rely on, and in his retinue he has some kings, some princes and a large number of chiefs and officers.
>
> Queen Neang Tieya is surrounded by a large court; several thousand servants daily carry out her wishes. Neither of the two is a stranger to me. The King is my father and the Queen my mother. There are two of us, Sauvirong and Vorvong. Saurivong is the elder. My father has a second wife, Neang Montea; he fulfills all her desires. She has a son, Vey Vongsa.
>
> Before this woman arrived, the King had never made our mother unhappy. But since Neang Montea could not stand the idea that my brother and I would be reigning later, she looked for an opportunity to destroy us. One day, we were

Figure 11

passing by her, she called us, held us very tight in her arms and shouted for help, accusing us of a crime against her very person.

The King did not want to hear any explanation; he gave way to anger and gave orders to the executioners who, at once, took us towards the forest to execute us. Our mother, moved by our complaints and our screams, followed our footprints, caught up with us and got the executioners to disobey the King's orders and managed to let us flee. She gave us each a precious ring and her kindest advice. She kissed us and, weeping, she returned to the palace heartbroken.

After having walked for months, dearly united and bearing our pain, helped only by her memory, one evening we arrived in the large kingdom of Conthop Borey. Exhausted, we spent the night in a house which we thought was there for travelers. When the hardhearted king heard about it, he got annoyed and had my brother taken away by officers and soldiers during our sleep.

I was woken up by the noise and fled into the woods. Since I couldn't find my beloved brother, I left that dreadful country behind me. I arrived here on a pitch-black night in a storm and stopped in front of the hut of a flower lady. Quite reluctantly she gave me shelter and a little rice and then, with harsh words, refused to lend me a torch.

Remembering the precious virtue of my mother's ring, I put it on my finger and a dazzling light sprang up and gave me light. The old lady noticed it and she ran to the palace to tell the King what a precious jewel I possessed.

I was arrested straightaway without anyone wanting to hear my story. Without being tried I was thrown into a cage and, for six years now, I have been coping with hunger, a cangue around my neck and chains around my ankle without anyone having mercy on me. My only support was the hope of seeing my dearest mother again and finding my brother who was lost.

And now, Princess, through you, the gods have come to help me. I entrust my fate to their wisdom and to your kindness.

Choked with tears, Neang Kessey returned indoors quickly. She prepared a sumptuous meal, went and served it to him with tender respect, and then filling his heart with hope, bowed, raising her hands together to her forehead, and walked home confidently.

That day, when the servants and the guards woke up they wondered what was the cause of such an unusually deep sleep.

Inside her palace the young girl was now thinking about Vorvong and she reproached herself for thinking he was just an ordinary man. Her eyes often swelled up and she exclaimed: "Noble and dear Vorvong, you will get a high rank in the world and your race will be the highest of all."

Let us change the subject and talk about the Kingdom of Chay Borey. Its powerful, fair and kind king was Sotat. Some wise chiefs ran his towns and his people enjoyed perfect happiness.

The King had a daughter; she was pretty, young, intelligent and incomparably kind. She was loved by everyone who approached her and she was surrounded by a lot of attention.

Sotat was King Thornit's friend and ally and their ambassadors or some messengers were constantly on their way from one to another.

One day, an ignorant, brutal and ferocious giant entered the kingdom. His arrival frightened the local spirit, the guardian of the country, so he abandoned his cave, his residence, and retired under a tree.

The giant entered the cave and blocked the entrance with stones. Then, in his roaring voice, he addressed the King, shouting:

> Dear King who is reigning here, do not forget this: 'My name is Yack[1] Sokali and my power is extreme and supernatural. I chased the spirit of your country away; he found refuge

1 Monsters feeding on human flesh. The ogres of our fairy tales.

far away under the foliage of a tree. I do not fear either you or your soldiers; nevertheless, I will not lay hands on anyone from your palace; I will not hurt the people. I only wish to eat you, King, and I have come here only for that reason.

King Chay Borey believed that the end was near for him. The giant terrified him so much that he thought: "I must call my friend King Thornit; I will ask him to take care of my beloved daughter, the Queen and my kingdom." He sent his fast messengers, saying to himself: "My poor body, you are being threatened by a sad end!"

As soon as Thornit heard the regrettable news, he ordered the immediate gathering of the army in order to save his friend without delay. The warriors arrived in huge numbers from everywhere. The vessels, in large numbers, were at once armed.

A problem arose. Once the Royal Vessel was repainted, polished and ready, they tried in vain to launch the boat but the architects and the carpenters admitted they were helpless.

At once the King, sounding horns and gongs, called everywhere on anyone who thought they could carry out this operation. If they succeeded, the reward that they would ask for would be granted straightaway: silver, gold, silk or any other precious thing.

No one answered the repeated and urgent calls. Filled with consternation the officers returned to the palace. Vorvong saw them from his cage and asked them: "Could you tell me the reason for your calls?" Without answering but calling him a "mad boy," they went to the King and did not conceal the fact that only the miserable captive in the cage had asked them a question.

Forthwith, the King sent them to fetch the prisoner. "If you manage to launch my vessel, you will be set free and rewarded."

Kneeling before the King, the prince said: "Honorable King,

pardon me. I would not brag that I will succeed, but urged by you, I would take on the challenge, and if success was in my favor, you could put it on the account of heaven. All I require are fragrant candles and three beautiful flags."

In the presence of the King in front of the numerous chiefs and warriors, in front of a huge crowd of people who had come to witness the scene, Vorvong, kneeling down, called on the angels and then with his little finger he pushed the vessel. **(Figure 12)**

By a celestial favor, thanks to the merits of his glorious race, and for the accomplishment of his destiny, the reluctant vessel slid slowly at the touch of his finger right to the middle of the waves.

The army being ready, the vessel unfurled her sails, sailed off and reached the port of Chay Borey.

Some huts for the soldiers were quickly built and the King then made his way to the capital where his friend Sotat explained the situation. "My dear faithful and best friend", he said, ending with and showing his despair, "The giant who has decided to make me perish is gigantic; he terrifies everybody." **(Figure 13)**

The King of Pohoul reassured him with these words: "Great and royal friend, banish all worries; let me save your life. One of my servants has a supernatural power; all by himself he launched my beautiful golden vessel into the sea."

Without delay he sent for Vorvong who had remained with the fleet.

But, Vorvong refused to go to him saying: "Before answering, I must know the cause, good or bad, of the King's appeal."

Thornit understood Vorvong's desire, which made him say: "I want to charge you to defeat Sukali, the threatening Giant who lives in a cave near the capital and wants the life of the

Figure 12

Figure 13

King"

The prince replied: "I agree to combat the yack instead of a sovereign, but if I were to succumb it should be as a prince. I request the royal insignia and clothes."

The King ordered that his wish be granted **(Figure 14).** Then, to escort him he sent his beautiful, brave and terrible war elephants.

When Vorvong arrived in the capital, dressed and adorned as a king and on the back of the royal elephant, he looked like the powerful Pra-En himself. **(Figure 15)**

Seeing this young prince with masculine and charming features inspiring confidence, the two sovereigns felt very happy.

King Sotat asked him to come close to the throne; then he said: "Brave Vorvong, I asked someone to beg you to combat the hardhearted giant. If you win, I will give you my throne and I will abdicate." **(Figure 16)**

Answering the hope of the King, Vorvong respectfully bowed and said:

"Mighty sovereign, I appeal to your kindness to be handed the sacred sword with the irresistible blade. With such a weapon, if the outcome of the fight is unfavorable to me, I will not regret not living."

After having pronounced these words, he called on the heavens, went towards the cave and, with a single kick of his foot, scattered all the rocks that were blocking the entrance. Seeing his courage, the angels were delighted, wished for his success and prayed so that he would get it.

In the presence of an opponent, undoubtedly the gods' protege, the frightened yack could not throw himself into the fight. Vorvong pulled out his sword and went forward to take his life.

Near death, the giant groveled in front of the victorious

Figure 14

Figure 15

Figure 16

man: "Strong lord, be magnanimous. Your destiny is that of Buddha; one day you will be the saviour of the world. Let me live, I am begging you, and I will immediately return to where I came from." **(Figure 17)**

King Sotat, being so pleased to see Vorvong coming back as the victor, couldn't take his eyes off of him and noticed the admirable ring shining on his finger:

> Dear Vorvong, I have no more doubts about your origins; this most precious stone shows that you were born into a glorious family. But even if your father was an ordinary man, your destiny is that of Buddha.
>
> Your courage and merit are well known to everyone. You have spared the country from misfortune, and not only have you saved the life of a king but also that of a father. I am placing in your hands my treasures, my crown, and the Kingdom, and I entrust you with the happiness of my daughter.

King Thornit informed him that he was doing him the same remarkable favor and with Nang Kessey, he was giving him his kingdom.

This important news was announced to the people in accordance with the practice, and the preparations for the raising of the triumphant person to the throne as well as his marrying the two princesses began straightaway.

The ceremonies took place at the said date. Some young, slim-waisted girls, chosen among the most beautiful ones in both countries, formed a retinue for the two charming queens. The Brahmans and the astrologists gathered together predicted their happiness and prosperity.

Joyous spectacles embellished the party, and they heard all kinds of music, cries of pleasure, joyful and confused noises.

After Vorvong had been raised to the throne of Chay Borey, King Thornit said his farewells to him as well as his daughter; then, he returned on his ship to the capital of Pohoul where happiness continued to prevail.

Figure 17.

Now king of two kingdoms, Vorvong was loved and respected by the people and envoys from all corners of his empire arrived to greet him.

One day, the spirit who had been chased out of the country by Yack Sokali came to pay homage to him. He presented him with a bright crystal ball which he was holding in his hand and said:

> This precious jewel will allow you, as a king, to fulfil your most beautiful wishes, and as long as you possess it your reign will be protected from enemies. In order to travel through space, all you will have to do is hold it in your hand.

Then he added:

> Dear King, here is the request I have come to make; when Yack Sokali forced me to leave my old home, I took refuge under a huge tree, the branches and leaves of which had useful and very rare qualities, but I can only be happy and content in my cave. Dear King, our saviour, allow me to return and live there.

The King replied: "Let it be so."

CHAPTER III - SEPARATION AND REUNION

After a year of reign, Queen Kessey, Rot Vodey's big sister, happened to have been with child for three months. Then the thought that her father was on his own, obsessed her; she lost her appetite and could not sleep. Vorvong agreed on making the journey she wanted.

The two queens were very fond of each other; they embraced one another constantly, each making recommendations until the departure. Then, with the marvelous crystal in his left hand, Vorvong tenderly embraced Kessey with his right arm; soon and without much effort they rose in the air and flew towards Pohoul.

When everyone had been informed of their departure, a general sadness hung over the country. The dignitaries, the officers, the people, all were worried; people were coming and going, weeping. Others were beating their chests, saying:

> Dear and generous King, why did you leave us on our own with our queen, without soldiers and servants? Which country did you go to through the air? If something happens to you, how will we be informed? We cannot be without you. Is it possible for our young queen to be alone? Should she have a war to withstand, how could we warn you?

Seeing the distress caused by the absence of her husband, Rot Vodey could not hold back her tears.

> My beloved, you left without an escort, without servants. You who were never deprived of anything; I am extremely worried knowing that you are far away. Why did you leave me on my own? I feel that I cannot bear the burden of isolation. Why can't I fly through the air and follow you?

Neang Kessey and Vorvong were shining in the sky like the queen of the nights. The first night, they covered thirty leagues. **(Figure 18)**

Figure 18

Catching sight of a hermitage on a desert island, the thought of stopping there came to them. They glided down to earth and went and greeted the hermit. **(Figure 19)**

Amazed to see them, the old man said to them: "Where have you come from? For five thousand years I have been praying on this island; I haven't seen a single human being. Did you arrive by sea or do you have the power of moving through space?"

With respect Vorvong bowed and replied:

> Venerable hermit, we have come from Chay Borey and we are going to Pohoul to visit our parents. A wonderful crystal ball allows us to fly. When we saw you on this island, we wanted to answer your wishes and your prayers. Lend us your basket and we will go to the meadow and fill it with flowers in order to make a bouquet for your holy altar.

Vorvong entrusted the hermit with his crystal ball, and, followed by Neang Kessey, walked away as light as a feather, picking flowers from all the trees. **(Figure 20)**

When they had gone, the old man looked at the precious object and considering stealing it, he thought:

> For so many centuries I have been praying with the aim of becoming able to fly through space. Five thousand entire years have passed, I will never again hold such a crystal ball with a beautiful jewel which this human being unsuspectingly asked me to look after.

He took the dazzling ball; his joy knew no bounds. He rose into space as far as he could climb, not knowing where he was going. Quickly he got lost and he found himself in the region of the terrible wind, Kamoreath. The whirlwind pushed him and in no time at all his body, in pieces, was thrown into the sea. This death was the fair punishment for the fault of the lonely hard-hearted man. **(Figure 21)**

The crystal ball fell onto the capital of Conthop Borey where Saurivong was reigning. It was laying on the ground, dazzling.

Figure 19

Figure 20

Figure 21

An officer saw it first and went and offered it to the King.

The same day, it was left in the safekeeping of the treasurer. **(Figure 22)**

Vorvong and Kessey returned, loaded with flowers which they arranged in pretty bouquets for the hermit.

Once they were ready to present him with them, they realised that he had vanished. Their disappointment was enormous when they could not see the crystal ball. The two young newlyweds emitted a similar cry of distress: "The hermit has taken our precious treasure and has run away! Is it possible that a religious man could have stolen our only resource?"

"Dear wife, I feel so sorry for you who has never experienced misery nor fatigue."

The young couple left the hermitage where the damned lonely man had lived. They wandered up hill and down dale, making their way at random. They came across a shelter and, despite their being disheartened, they were pleased to have found a place to rest.

A yack who was residing there soon found out about the arrival on the island of two human beings. Attracted by their smell, he shouted from outside the hut, waving his terrible stick endlessly, thinking: "What audacious humans may be so daring as to take my refuge? In a minute I am going to show them how humans can perish."

Boldly, Vorvong replied: "Ignorant and rude yack, you don't know how superior to you I am in terms of strength and power." Angels, who were called on through a short prayer, put some terror inside the giant who bowed and went away thinking to himself: "Where can this supernatural man be from? How can I make him perish?" But he dared not to come back **(Figure 23).**

The young king put his arms around his wife and said: "Let us leave, my beloved; this place is dangerous. We couldn't

Figure 22

Figure 23

constantly protect ourselves from the yack; we would become his prey."

When dawn dispersed the darkness, they found themselves on a boundless sea shore. They could only hear the murmur of the wind and the roaring of the waves. In front of this barrier the prince's eyes were wandering, full of sadness and grief, until the moment he got in sight of the shore and spotted some tree trunks able to bear both their weights floating on the water. They managed to reach them and jumped on them. **(Figure 24)**

A fortuitous wind then pushed them not far from the coast on the opposite side. Without doubt, it was his time to atone for an offence from a previous life.

A horrific storm arrived unexpectedly and the sky got so dark that the prince could not see anything under its thick curtain. The waves became furious. The unfortunate couple were not able to withstand them and, in spite of their efforts, they got separated.

The princess, exhausted and thrown about by the waves, rolled onto the beach. Being hurt, she dragged herself, called Vorvong and wandered around. Then, feeling exhausted, she fell down on her knees, asking:

> My beloved, are you on the beach or in the water? Were you the prey of ferocious sea monsters? On the shore, aren't you also exposed to the beasts?
>
> Dear spirits who inhabit the seas and the beaches, have mercy on my crying. Have you seen my beloved Vorvong? Tell me where I may find him. I want to follow him and always serve him. Dear angels who inhabit the seven directions and watch over the woods and forests, the earth, the seas and the air, the world, the sky even, tell me where he is. I want to join him.
>
> O immense forests and you green trees which grow in pairs with flowers blooming, are you going to gaze at my terrible pain without intervening? When an implacable fate is

Figure 24

tearing from my love half of my being, my beloved prince, are you not going to be affected by my sorrow and loneliness; are you not going to help me? I want to find him again; otherwise, I pray you, cause me to die!

She kept on calling, praying, moaning until she was exhausted and she remained on the sand, lifeless; she had fainted. When she regained consciousness, her entire body was fatigued and painful. She got up, stopped crying, pulled her scarf off her chest and used it as a flag, a signal, by putting it at the end of a branch which she planted in the sand. **(Figure 25)**

Despite being three months pregnant, she walked continuing to search the woods and the ravines. Her wounded feet were leaving bloody footprints behind her on the path. Soon, she lost her way and being completely exhausted, she stopped and lied down under the foliage of a big tree agitated by a light wind.

The forest was huge, thick and uneven. Neang Kessey walked everywhere through it for four months being under the constant impression that she was threatened by beasts and therefore not daring to utter a word. She then found herself on the border of the kingdom where Saurivong was reigning. Gradually her clothes got torn by thorns and the undergrowth, and then she had to cover her body with leaves.

The direction she was following, without being aware of it, was the way to the capital. In a village, not too far away, there lived an old man, a skilled hunter. A group of dogs usually followed him on his adventures. As weapons, he had a spear and a bow and his quiver was full of sharp arrows. That day, as usual, walking along the fields, he followed the forest. Suddenly, the dogs set off towards a human being awkwardly dressed; it was Neang Kessey. The noisy barking of the dogs guided the hunter. The poor young girl fled using all the strength she had left. When the dogs were close to reaching her, a steep ditch appeared in front of her and she let herself slide down into it. **(Figure 26)**

Figure 25

Figure 26

Thinking that he was dealing with ordinary game, the old man hurried, guided by the dogs barking, but just as he was arming his bow he saw the young lady. "Maybe", he thought, "some spirit is testing my old experience. "Are you", he said, "a spirit of the woods or a human creature?"

"Where can you be coming from dressed in leaves? You look unhappy. Why are you on your own?"

> Good old man, my husband and I capsized not far from the coast and the furious waves separated us. I pray you, take in a poor unfortunate person, have mercy on her and her sorrow. I will be your servant and do my best to make you happy as a gesture of thanks for that good deed. When I find my husband again, he will reward you, I can assure you, for your generous heart.

The old man said: "Don't worry anymore; I will provide you with all you need." With his big knife he cut a branch off a tree and put it in the ditch to be used as a ladder. Then he threw some of his clothes to the young lady. Seeing that he wanted to help her, Neang Kessey swiftly put the clothes on and climbed up along the branch.

Pleased with his kindness, the old hunter took her to his house without thinking about hunting anymore.

When his wife saw the two of them arrive, her nasty and jealous eyes filled up with anger and she turned her back on them.

"Miserable old man", she shouted, "your skin is shriveling up and you still have a lover? No doubt to hide it from me, you built a hut for her in the forest, and now that a child is about to be born, you are bringing her here; you are so naive."

> Listen, woman, be polite and don't speak nasty and hopeless words. Will you ever be fair and kind? At least wait until you hear what I have to tell you. This unfortunate lady whom a shipwreck separated from her husband, arrived on her own. I took pity on her and I brought her here to give her some food until she finds the one she has lost. So, stop say-

ing that she has come to steal my feelings for you.

But the old woman did not let him finish. Addressing Neang Kessey, she said: "You are going to learn how I treat people who give advice. Miserable old man, you took advantage of this child and the judges will punish you. You will pay the penalty; your neck will soon be trapped in a cangue and your head will fall one day; it is certain!" **(Figure 27)**

Whilst she was talking, she became furious; She threw herself onto the old man, grabbed his hair, and with her nails, pulled out the flesh on his face. Nothing could calm her down.

Then she turned around to the young lady and said: "As for you, shameless and wayward heart who is able to have such a passing fancy, robber of husbands pretending to be astonished, get out of here; you are bringing shame upon my house!"

With her great kindness, the poor victim reckoned: "If she wants to kill me, I won't be able to defend myself, but the angels will not want to let me die. I shall not leave this good man before I have found my husband: I will show him my gratitude by bearing whatever pains I will have to suffer."

In the pitch-black night and despite the rain, the old woman left her lying on the damp ground at the bottom of her hut.

Neang Kessey arrived at the tenth month of her pregnancy still being a miserable servant until, on a furiously stormy day, she felt some labour pains. So she begged the old woman: "Mistress, allow me to tell you the truth: my child is about to come into this world, I desperately need to be assisted." "

"Get away from me! Get out at once! I don't have any children and I couldn't bear such a scene."

"Please, let me stay in the enclosed plot of land, at the base of your hedge, I cannot go anywhere in this rain, in this thunder."

"Go onto the path!" She pushed her back, opened the gate

Figure 27

and threw her out.

Neang Kessey looked for a path that she could follow. The pain forced her to sit down on the ground. Tears were flowing down her emaciated face.

> My beloved, do you happen to be dead? If your life was saved, let me know where you are so that I can go and find you and serve you until my dying day! If someone told me that you were at the bottom of the sea, I would let myself die; why on earth would I live if I did not have any hope of finding you?

By a favor of heaven, Pra En, with his sharp and merciful eyes, saw the situation the young woman was in. In the features of a good old lady, he went to her and said: "Young and charming lady, what are you doing here in such appalling weather?"

> Good woman, I have been separated from my husband in a storm, I lost my way looking for him, I had to work as a servant in the house of a hunter whose nasty wife insulted me, ill-treated me and because she did not want to see me giving birth to my child, has just kicked me out of the house. Good woman I am suffering unbearable pain and I cannot breathe anymore.

She thought she was dying. In tears, she murmured a gentle prayer to the angels:

> My misery was part of destiny. Pitiless fate, you took my husband from me and you are mysteriously hiding him from me. If he is alive, I want to live and find him; if he is no more, let me die and join him in the next life so that nothing can keep us apart anymore! Let me be a bird with wings always ready to fly through the air if he is one too. I will only be happy next to him. Let me be a wild beast if he is one too. If he is a fish, I want to be one too. Beyond this death I will be happy only if I have been reunited with him. Hear my prayer, dear celestial angels, and satisfy my last wishes!

She turned around to the old woman and said: "Good lady, save my child, save my life; this kindness will be equal to the one I owe my mother."

Holding her shoulders, the god said: "Do not worry anymore; I will not leave you."

Neang Kessey gave birth to a beautiful boy. When Pra En saw him, he said: "He will be my grandson!" **(Figure 28)**

He produced a fire, warmed up the young mother and then he said:

> My house is in the eastern part of the palace, I will take your beautiful child with me and take good care of him. When you are able to come and see him, you will find him again. Do not worry. Give me an object which, put around his neck, will identify him. You are on your own and without aid, at your nasty mistress's you would not find one moment to devote to him and he could not live in those conditions.

"Good woman, thank you. I entrust you with my child; love him and take good care of him as if you yourself had given birth to him. When I have found my husband again, we will come and get him and we will reward you for your priceless caring."

In her arms she took the child who was born in such miserable conditions and shed tears on him:

> Sweet precious treasure of my heart, it is so difficult and painful to part with you; what could a poor servant do? My selfish mistress would cause your death and so, for fear of seeing you unhappy, I put you in the care of this good lady. We shall see each other again. In one month I will leave my master, I will go and take care of you, and there will be the two of us to love you.

Having so said, she handed the precious load to the old woman and entrusted her with her husband's ring.

When Neang Kessey returned to the hunter's house, his wife asked: "So, miserable girl, did you abandon your child?" **(Figure 29)**

"You didn't wish to see him, so I put him in the care of a charitable person who adopted him as her grandson."

Once the young mother had gone, Pra En placed the child

Figure 28

Figure 29

on a superb carpet and tied his mother's ring around his neck. He turned into a vulture which by spreading out its wings could protect itself from the rain, the dew and the sun.

King Saurivong, the long time sovereign of Conthop Borey, having expressed the desire to go for a ride at the edge of the forest very early in the morning. He put on his insignia and his crown and went out on the royal elephant's back followed by a large escort and was greeted and admired by the respectful crowd. As he went past the hunter's hut, his eyes were attracted by the vulture which, in spite of the escort approaching, under its spread-out wings kept an attitude of proud indifference.

"Someone go and looks at what the vulture is eating!"

An officer rushed to obey the command of the King. The vulture jumped, moved out of the way and the officer saw the child.

> Dear king, an abandoned beautiful newly born baby, similar to those of the angels. is lying there on a superb cloth. The vulture was going to take his life when we turned up; surely without us this delightful creature would have been devoured.

Pleased with such an encounter, Saurivong ordered: "Bring him to me quickly, I want to see him." **(Figure 30)**

Delicately, someone presented him to the King, who received him in his arms. "I am adopting this beautiful child." He caressed him, admired him and noticed the ring attached at his neck. He compared it with his and was amazed as well as puzzled to find they were similar. He had no doubt that he was holding his brother's child in his arms.

> Dear child, what good fortune puts you in my hands; but why are you on your own? Where is your father? Strange destiny, a consequence of our previous lives, why these violent and painful separations?

He abandoned himself to the sorrow which gnawed at his heart and tears flowed down in the surroundings. The escort

Figure 30

scattered around in vain but no one thought about asking the people in the miserable hut.

The King then returned to the palace which had skillful child-minders among the pretty and elegant ladies he had selected. He ordered that a smart four room house be built at once for the little prince in the main courtyard and that it be decorated with murals featuring the scenes of his own youth which he lived with his brother. With sounding gongs and trumpets he announced that he would inaugurate it with a superb feast and that, on that occasion, he would distribute huge riches, that the whole crowd would be allowed in the little palace where all the visitors would be accommodated and to whom, guards carefully chosen, would explain the scenes painted on the walls.

When everything was ready, he asked the guards afterwards to come and tell him the impressions that the paintings had produced in the visitors.

Let us now get back to poor Vorvong!

Violently separated from his young wife, he fought for his life against the furious waves. After some desperate efforts he reached the coastline. He looked for her, searching in vain the folds of the ground and the hidden areas of the shoreline. Abandoning himself to grief, he cried:

> My beloved treasure, what have we done to deserve so much misfortune? Why didn't I refuse to make this journey?
>
> I wish I knew where you were; I could join you! Did you die drowning in the sea? Have you been eaten by sea monsters? Are you lost in dark forests? Were you the prey of ferocious animals? Could it be possible, by chance, that you were taken in by a charitable hunter?

The unfortunate prince was going along the shore, feeling sad and only the roaring of the waves was answering his calls. All of a sudden, on a remote beach, he noticed a signal, a flag.

He quickened his pace, shaking with hope, as if the piece of cloth floating in the wind was going to bring back his beloved to him. He recognised Neang Kessey's scarf and saw her footprints in the sand. **(Figure 31)**

The wound in his heart intensified even more.

> My dear treasure, destiny took you onto this beach, but you left nothing but your scarf and your footprints! No doubt you took only the time to put this light cloth, symbol of hope, at the tip of this branch! Dear scarf, you who covered my beloved, you are the only souvenir of our separation! Oh, solitudes, tell me about her sorrow! Is she lost in your creases? Have pity on her and her suffering! You had the most precious pieces of cloth in abundance, your fatigue was due to the entertainment at the palace, you were surrounded by people caring for you as much as the angels. Now you are walking half naked in the hot sun through interminable forests.

Exhausted, the prince fainted on the sand covered with Kessey's footprints. When he got up, he followed these still fresh footprints and reached the edge of the forest; but there the soil was carpeted with grass. It was impossible for him to recognise any footprints. He called for a long time and only echos answered him. For six months he searched all over the forest; it held no secret for him anymore; it was hopeless.

One day he happened to be in the fields and arrived at the capital of Canthop Borey, feeling sad. He overheard that the King was giving a big party and that he had ordered the distribution of abundant alms in the courtyard of the palace for the inauguration of a house and that on its walls were scenes featuring his childhood. "Let me go in", he said to himself; "I will get my share of the King's alms and I will see the paintings."

In accordance with the orders that the officers had received, when they saw him they let him in, presented him with all kinds of goods, gave him new clothes and invited him to have a meal. Then they accompanied him to have a look at the paintings.

Figure 31

They described the scenes to him in detail.

First there was the happy and tranquil childhood of the King and his brother with their mother.

As they were talking, Vorvong realised that the topics were those of his own life. He was seized by emotion and fell on his knees, thinking:

> What incredible fate; here I am being featured playing with my brother near my mother during a period of happiness! Here, Neang Montea is holding us in her arms! That other picture shows the King being angry and ordering that we be murdered! Here is our terrible walk towards the forest with the executioners. Our mother, panicking, rushes to join us! The executioners, on their knees, surprised and moved, let us go! There, it is our passing among the saleswomen of the country of Baskim! The large tree on the branch of which we rested on the first night! The roosters fighting, one morning! The white rooster and the black one which was exhausted, both dying in the end! The fire we lit in order to grill their flesh, before setting off! Finally, our stop in the hut in the wood where my dear brother was kidnapped!
>
> Guards, which one among you will be able to show me to my beloved brother?

The sobs were blinding and suffocating him. The officers left him on the floor and sneaked out, knowing enough. They hurried, pleased to be going to tell the King what they had seen **(Figure 32):**

> A poor stranger, young, handsome, looking like you, our King, like your person, presented himself at the palace. We gave him all the necessities and once he had had his meal, we took him to see the paintings.
>
> We were then about to describe them to him; but he understood; he fell on the floor crushed with emotion and fainted.

Saurivong rushed to him, recognised his brother and embraced him.

> My dearest brother, partner of my pains, during the long months that I lost you, my existence has been filled with sad-

Figure 32

ness. There was not a single day when I was not thinking about you. My dear treasure whom I was constantly expecting to see again, at last the generous heaven is reuniting us!

Tears of joy were flowing.

At the same time, Vorvong was overcome with joy and gradually the tears relieved his anguish. He told his brother about the misery he had suffered. "Beloved brother, I don't know how I am still alive."

He recounted the story of his ring, the only souvenir he had kept from his mother and because of which he suffered six years of martyrdom. He narrated the launching of the vessel, the victory over the giant, his crowning and his marriage, the journey through the air, the descent onto the island, the theft by the hermit, the shipwreck and the separation.

> Dearest brother, you are my saviour, it is thanks to you that I will be able to see our dear mother again. I wondered if you were dead. Your kidnapping had me fearing the worst. I would never have thought that I would find you as the King of this beautiful country.
>
> After so many pains, I am experiencing a gentle joy in looking at you! But alas, an unequaled sorrow is mixed with this; I have lost my beloved wife. She has probably suffered so many miseries that I am so shaken and I fear that she may have succumbed. When the furious waves separated us, she had already been pregnant for three months and I have been mourning her loss for seven months.

"Listen, dear brother", Sauvirong said:

> I found a newly born boy on a path lying on a rich carpet. Hanging around his neck was a wonderful ring. That child is not foreign to our blood line; he is certainly your son. The ring made me realize this. Having in vain until now, searched everywhere to find you, I had the idea of the room with the paintings and asked the officers to announce that I would, for its inauguration, give a party and generous alms.
>
> Some guards were in charge of relating the story of my life to everyone and giving the details of our long misery. It is through this means, thanks to heaven, that I have been able

to be reunited with my beloved brother.

"Dear brother", Vorvong asked, "Satisfy my impatience; I wish to see the child you are raising."

Straightaway, the little prince was brought in, surrounded by childminders and servants.

When Vorvong saw the child with the ring hanging from his neck, he recognised him, took him lovingly and shed some tears.

> Dear child whom, owing to the angels, today I can tenderly hold in my arms, why were you abandoned on the road? Dear little one, where can your mother be? This dear treasure of mine, I fear for her life; might she have been captured by men without heart or mercy?

This thought caused him so much pain that he fainted. Saurivong, frightened by his brother's state, moistened his face with cool water and brought him back to life.

The unfortunate Princess Kessey at the service of her mistress was, despite her good will, constantly ill-treated and insulted. Every day that merciless old woman threatened to kick her out. After seven days, she left her mistress and went looking for her child. She headed for the palace and entered it without being cautious.

While looking for the good woman's hut, she wandered near the house built for her child. Vorvong, at the entrance of the room, was looking sadly outside. He saw Neang Kessey, recognised her as she was walking away and rushed towards her. He held her by her belt and hugged her. Soon she was soaked with his tears. **(Figure 33)**

In no time at all they told each other their misfortunes. Vorvong pulled her into the house, telling her how his brother had taken in their son.

Neang Kessey picked up the child and covered him with kisses and caresses.

Figure 33

> Blessed be the destiny which makes me see you again. I thank the angels who had wanted that the King, your uncle, take care of you and your father. We are now united forever. You, precious treasure of my heart! I have not seen your face for seven days. I had thought that the good old woman would raise you. She had asked me to have you as her grandson. I can't understand how she was able to abandon you in the middle of the road and how a vulture protected you under its wing! Instead, wasn't I aided by an angel under the appearance of an old woman?

When she dried her tears of joy, the two kings, the two brothers, took her to Queen Sar Bopha who welcomed her with extreme delight. Saurivong ordered the celebration of a superb ceremony on the occasion of the happy return of his brother and his family. Then, during a big party, the pretty name Vorvong Sauria was given to the child under the applause of the dignitaries and the people who had come to greet him.

CHAPTER IV - THE BATTLE OF KINGS

"Beloved brother," said Saurivong one day, "you did not mention again your wonderful crystal; I am eager to see it. One day, I was offered a dazzling beautiful ball and I kept it. Could it be the one you lost?"

Full of hope, Vorvong asked to see it and so some officers brought it in. "It is my very jewel, good brother; if you allow me, I will show you its power straightaway."

Taking it in his hand, he tossed it around and it soared upwards into the air, flew around the enclosure, tracing big circles around the palace and then landed at the feet of King Saurivong. Everyone who saw this was amazed. The whole town was excited and wanted to watch this. **(Figure 34)**

Vorvong bowed respectfully and said:

> Dear brother, our beloved mother advised us to be back in ten years' time. She is thinking about us all the time. Let us not forget her advice and let us have pity on her pain. If you do not mind, I will go back and get all that is needed from my kingdoms. It is here that I will join you; we only take the time necessary to prepare the vessels."

Saurivong replied: "Your idea is good. I am going to organise an army so that we can arrive from both sides at the same time and ensure success, because as soon as people find out about our route, obstacles will be put in place."

Vorvong added: "I give to you the care of Neang Kessey and my child, dear brother. I am very concerned since they have been so unfortunate!"

Then he said his good-byes to his wife in these terms:

> Dear Kessey, most charming of all women, I am going to leave you to go back to the kingdom. Poor Rot Vodey must be worried after such a long absence; she must be feeling very sad. Do not regret my departure and do not make your

Figure 34

days unhappy. I would like to take you with me and never be parted from you again but the fear of an accident affects me. I am going to use the crystal ball again. My absence devoted to preparing for the return of our mother will be short. I will come back with Rot Vodey and I will bring back more servants.

Having pronounced those words, he rose into the air. His elegant flight was like that of Hansa, the bird of heaven, taking its flight from the beautiful gardens of good celestial regions. **(Figure 35)**

It took only one day for Vorvong to reach his capital. He embraced Rot Vodey, who tenderly narrated her pains and her worry during their separation.

Vorvong told her about his journey with Neang Kessey, their shipwreck, and the miseries they suffered being separated. Generous Vodey wept; she was so moved and sorry. Then the young couple went to visit the old king. They were much welcomed.

Dear child, every day we were invaded by the grief of your absence! Feeling impatient, we spent so much time talking about your return; we so much felt the need to hold and love you! Where did you leave our charming Kessey? Is she feeling happy or sad? Did she forget us, for she has not taken advantage of your return to come and see us!

Vorvong recounted the story of his miseries and King Sotat could not hold back his tears. **(Figure 36)**

Soon Vorvong resumed his journey; he headed towards the country of King Thornit. **(Figure 37)**

To his father-in- law he recounted his misfortunes, then said to him: "Honourable King, I have come to ask you for five hundred vessels and an army to go against my native country."

King Thornit said: "This kingdom is yours; your wish will be satisfied."

Vorvong embarked with the soldiers, carefully selected, re-

Figure 35

Figure 36

Figure 37

turned to King Sotat and put the same request to him.

Promptly the troops were raised and the fleet was equipped.

Then Vorvong said to his father-in-law: "Grand and generous King, I am making fervent wishes for the fortune of your kingdom. My absence will be short. I would like to ask your permission to take your dear daughter, my wife, with me, so that she can meet my dear mother."

King Sotat would have preferred to keep his lovely Rot Vodey near him, but he did not dare to refuse.

> My dearest son, I can't upset your plans - go. May the heavens protect you, but do not leave us for too long in loneliness. Do not forget that your presence here is indispensable, that your elevation to the throne of the kingdom was the happiest event in my life. You were the man chosen to save our race.

Then, addressing his daughter, he said:

> Treasure of my life, you whom I love more than anything else, listen to my wise recommendations. Take care of your husband, respect and obey him always. When you have safely arrived in his country, serve his parents as if they were your own. May nothing make you seem foreign in their eyes. Pay attention to the spirits of the countries where you happen to be. Be kind and gentle to those who will serve you.
>
> Reduce the misery of the unfortunate ones. Love those whom your husband will love, do not diminish his happiness through jealousy. In all things, exercise kindness and moderation. For those who will be subjected to your husband's disgrace, do not have the same feeling as him; be kind and speak for them to the King. When your husband, during the night, will come into your room, lie down slightly lower than him; do not remain at an equal level.

Having received this advice from her father with respect, the young princess saluted him kneeling.

The fleet headed at full sail for Conthop Borey, where it was warmly welcome by Saurivong, who received his brother transported into his palace. **(Figure 38)**

Figure 38

When they met again, Neang Kessey and Rot Vodey threw themselves into each other's arms and kept on chatting. Rot Vodey picked up little Prince Vorvong Sauria. She tenderly sat him on her lap and covered him with kisses and caresses. The thought of the misfortune he had suffered made her shed tears. **(Figure 39)** "Dear child, the protection of heaven is over you; without it you would not have been able to resist so much affliction."

"At last we have been reunited," said Vorvong. "Dear brother, let us carry out our plan; let us leave for our parents' kingdom."

Saurivong replied: "You take command of the fleets and I will lead the army. We will calculate our progression so that we enter our father's kingdom at the same time and suddenly block the capital."

The final preparations for leaving were advanced and could not wait for a favorable day.

In both armies, order and discipline prevailed. Saurivong formed the vanguard with his most courageous men. He chose his officers from among those who showed great courage; they carried their swords over their shoulders and their headdresses had bright colors. The army was innumerable. The ground shook under their feet and among the happy warriors, each could only think of seizing the opportunity to demonstrate his value. All one could see were flags and banners of all sorts flapping in the wind.

Saurivong took the Queen with him; a crowd of splendid women formed her retinue. Nothing was missing; everything had been planned. The army set off in several separate troops in perfect order. The road was going to be long and difficult, and so Saurivong was eager to arrive.

Vorvong, for his part, organized the fleet. It was composed

Figure 39

of experienced sailors whose courage and bravery were their ordinary qualities. A considerable amount of supplies filled up the vessels. Flags and multicolored banners were flying at the tops of the masts. A carefully chosen troop formed the King's guard.

The fleet was innumerable; all one could see was a forest of masts and rudders. It set off at the same time as the army. A vessel with magnificent sculptures and adorned with beautiful garlands of flowers carried the young king and the queens. While sailing away, the three, together with Saurivong and Sar Bopha, mounted on superb elephants, exchanged best wishes. **(Figure 40)**

Soon one could only hear the howling of the wind, the waves rising high and coming down, beating heavily on the planking of the vessels. One could see only the limitless stretch of the water and the sky.

In the evening, the fleet anchored at an island. The seamen restored their strength by eating abundantly. All of them, leaning over the side of the vessel and in the light of the moon and the stars, admired all kinds of sea animals. The next day, they resumed sailing.

Let us leave the armies' progression and let us talk about King Sauriyo and Queen Tieya, the father and the mother of Saurivong and Vorvong. After Vorvong and Saurivong, the children rescued from death, had fled, what happened? Since the King was exasperated by Neang Tieya's grief, he threw her out of the palace. In her rejection, the poor queen owed her life soley to the sympathetic executioners who would daily, in secret, bring her the necessities to maintain her life: rice, betel and wood. Fearing the anger of the King, nobody dared to rescue her.

Figure 40

Seven years later, Vey Vongsa in his twelfth year had become the sacred King in place of his father who had abdicated. He governed five hundred dependent principalities; annually, treasures, riches and precious objects of all kinds were presented to him.

Prosperity and well-being continued to prevail with the populations of his empire; however, time was passing. The unfortunate abandoned Queen Tieya had advised her sons to come back after ten years without fail. Despite her courage, she was still affected by the worry and the sadness which their departure left in her. The only companions of her misery were sorrow, pain, suffering and the impatience for seeing her children again.

One night, however, she had this charming dream. Both her sons came back, embellished with youth and health. They threw themselves at her feet, overwhelmed with pain when they saw how far into misery she had fallen. She held them tightly in her arms. They happy to see her again and she thrilled to have them returned, the three of them could not stop crying for joy and happiness. Suffocated with emotions, she woke up with a start, still trying to hug her children. The deep darkness brought her back to reality; she fell back into her pain and despair, tears soaked her body and she bitterly bemoaned: "My dear adorable children, I am so unhappy, I am everyday overwhelmed by grief. Since you left, ten years have passed and my misery is dreadful. I only owe my existence to the generosity of the executioners."

That day, at dawn, an innumerable army invaded the kingdom and marched on the capital.

There was nothing but terror and disorder among the people. The King was informed by some couriers who had been eyewitnesses of the invasion. "Honourable King, a huge army is invading the country; nothing can stop their audacious march."

Others rushed in saying: "Another army is arriving by sea. All we can see are vessels and warriors. Save us from a catastrophe, honourable King!"

King Vey Vongsa at once gathered his army. His warriors, always ready, were brave and well armed.

The news was then that the enemy had reached the capital and the royal residence was going to be surrounded. "All of you," King Vey Vongsa said, "officers and warriors, whatever their audacity, that enemy army will not be able to defeat us."

The armies of the two brothers gathered together. Vorvong, dressed for battle, went to his elder brother's tent. Surrounded by generals, officers and experts, the two kings took their place on the platform which had been quickly built in the middle of the huge troops' camp. Right away they chose some envoys to go to the old king. "Go to King Sauriyo and tell him we want his kingdom, his crown and its riches. If he refuses, invite him to war; we will impose it by the powerful force of our armaments." **(Figure 41)**

The envoys left and they took the request of the two kings to King Sauriyo. In hearing them, the old king burst out with cries of despair. "If I am defeated, I will perish by their weapons." In his terror, no thought of resistance came to his mind.

The heavens made him pay the consequences of his acts under the influence of Neang Montea, his second wife, towards his two children. He addressed the young King Vey Vongsa and said to him:

> Dear child, my saviour, what should I decide in front of this enemy? Should I agree to his wish? How could we find enough soldiers to engage in a battle with him? The Kingdom is in his hands and our people under his orders. A tragic fight will have terrible consequences for the country; it will result in our deaths. It is better if we surrender; at least the enemy will spare our lives.

Vey Vongsa replied:

Figure 41

Dear father, have no fear about the fate of the country. It is true that the enemy army is innumerable, that the Kingdom is in his hands, that the strength of his weapons is fearsome and that his soldiers are brave; but, we can still have a confrontation with them like with any other. I can be beaten and crushed, but you cannot make me withdraw without fighting. If the fate of the weapons is favorable to us, we will hold on to our kingdom; otherwise, we will agree to give it to our enemies. (**Figure 42)**

"Dear child, your views on fighting make me fear for your life. Since you choose to give battle to the enemy, tell the envoys to go and inform their king."

And so, Vey Vongsa announced:

Lords, you can go and tell your kings that we have no idea what the reason for their request is; we do not understand it. Tell them that we accept the battle and that I leave my destiny to the care of the weapons. In order to spare a bloodshed and lamentation, I request that there be a combat of elephants. Each army will choose the best that they have and your chief and I will mount them ourselves.

The envoys having listened carefully, respectfully took their leave from the young king and returned to their camp.

The two allied brothers were pleased with their adversary's suggestion. Right away Vorvong bowed in front of his elder brother and said: "Dear brother, I request the honor of the combat."

Saurivong replied: "Let your will be done." Vorvong nodded approvingly and said:

I assure you of my success, beloved brother. I do not fear a combat on elephants; I want to prove my strength and my skill. Have no worry; I will take our father's kingdom and I will give it to you.

I want you to stay on this platform; from here you will be able to watch the fight against Vey Vongsa.

At once Vorvong's escort was assembled and his warriors, dressed for combat, came to hear the priests praying for their

Figure 42

victory.

Vey Vongsa gave his orders and organized the necessary preparations. He went to say farewell to the King, asked what his wishes were and returned to his house. He adorned himself with all the royal ornaments and put on his head the crown covered with precious stones and gleaming with light and beauty. On his belt hung a sword with a handle made of gold studded with diamonds. On his fingers were some shiny rings and the hook of his stick was made of solid gold.

Once he had changed into his combat outfit, he mounted his elephant, which had new and shiny harnesses. **(Figure 43)**

Both armed men were superb in their pride and courage. A group of determined combatants formed the escort. The two allied brothers were on the platform surrounded by their ministers and a crowd of generals and chiefs. Then the approaching of the enemy was announced to them.

Saurivong commanded: "Order all the troops to take their positions, elephants and cavalry; prepare all of our weapons!"

Terrifying groups started to move and right away the King was informed of the execution of his orders.

Vorvong bowed and climbed on his elephant. His hands held magnificent weapons; a hook made of gold adorned one arm and a blade the other; the royal umbrella shaded his face.

The numerous selected escort, which went to combat at his side, advanced in an orderly manner. All one could see was a forest of weapons.

This march of warriors towards the enemy was accompanied by music, gongs and trumpets. The troops joined in and all of a sudden the fight began. All that could be heard were confused noises, shouting and weapons clashing. The ground was shaking under their steps. Not a single weapon remained still. The soldiers came together, attacked and defended them-

Figure 43

selves with swords and spears. Every which way there were some wounded men, victors and casualties. Men fell, knocked over, and others came to cut their throats. The warriors' feet were red; they were covered in blood.

The thick curtain of combatants thinned out, the space cleared up and the two kings launched their elephants towards one another. Their best warriors with them fought with spears, swords and pikes. All those blades flared up; one could see them tainted with blood, coming down and going up.

As soon as they collided, the elephants of the two kings tore each other apart. Without uttering a word their masters exchanged glances and crossed swords with each other.

The masculine features of their young faces expressed courage, calm and determination. Vey Vongsa was skillful and valiant, a superb king in combat and clever in his attacking. But soon Vorvong, invincible, with a quick strike of his long weapon cut off his adversary's head with his crown still on. **(Figure 44)**

At the sight of the dead king, the bravest of Vey Vongsa's guards stepped back and fear crept in among them. Like a moving wave they rolled out of the battlefield; one could see men fall down, shaking with fear and dying of exhaustion.

Vorvong gave the order by shouting at the defeated king's men to stop fleeing, not to be frightened, that he was sparing their lives. Bowing, with his hands joined on his forehead to the corpse of his brave adversary, he gave the orders so that they regarded him with respect.

Then the banners were raised. Vorvong gathered his soldiers all around them, went and bowed in front of his brother Suarivong to announce his victory.

Figure 44

CHAPTER V - JUSTICE AND RECONCILIATION

The two kings sent their father the news of his son's death:

> Tell him this: Glorious King, your brave son, abandoned by his good fortune, succumbed valiantly.
>
> Our glorious masters are asking you if you intend to carry on fighting. If so, go to the plateau and wait for them. If you don't want to, you can greet them in their camp. You will have to go there on foot and not on an elephant or other animal's back, unarmed and without escort; otherwise your attitude will be regarded as hostile and menacing and will provoke a new combat, the outcome of which will be fatal for you. You will pay for your temerity with your life.

When the old king heard this commanding language, he was scared and said:

> You, envoys of my strong adversaries! Why would I engage in a battle in which I would be defeated; my son has been betrayed by fate and he met with his death; there is nothing I can do anymore against them. I ask them to be generous and give me until tonight so that I can collect the gifts which I will take with me. I will hand over to them the kingdom and the treasures which I possess. I am only asking them to spare my life in return.

The envoys gave the two kings Sauriyo's reply. Right away the army received the following order:

> Let us have planted in the soil the flags, the banners, the emblems of all the troops and of all the chiefs. When the defeated king comes to greet the kings, we will not show him the Royal Platform, but we will keep abusing him. We will send him from flag to flag indicating the camps of chiefs, generals, ministers, all the way from the first one to the last one until his fatigue is extreme. Only then, once exhausted and not able to stand up, will he be taken to the allied kings. Let the music, the gongs and the trumpets sound loudly everywhere!

By giving that sort of order, the two brothers thought:

We will have him, for a while, suffer the misery which we suffered during long years. It is a miracle we are still alive. Without the help of heaven, our bodies would be buried in some dark forest. He has to feel the lesson and only when he is succumbing to suffering, will we receive him.

When the envoys had delivered their message, the old King Sauriyo was assailed by a thousand thoughts, and desperate, he burst into tears. He was afraid of dying and was mourning his son, his only support. Heart broken, he could not exist anymore.

Oh, dear child, my precious treasure, why did a fatal destiny take you away, so young, from my love? You, gentle consolation of my old days, never until now have you caused me pain. I gave you my kingdoms and you were the joy of my people! There were the two of us, my son and I; now I am alone! Why did you die so young in the middle of combat, with no parent near you to help you? I haven't even seen your face!

Your death has taken away from me my loved one, my saviour; it has ruined my life!

Neang Montea's grief was immense when she heard the terrible news; her chest was about to burst and her heart was beating so fast. **(Figure 45)**

My darling, my treasure, I am feeling an intolerable pain; I will never be able to get over this. Why is it that you, the joy of the people, have been violently taken by death? Why didn't I die with you? Why didn't you die in my womb when you had not developed yet, when you did not have all my love, when you were not a king?

She could not stop mourning her son; her body was shaking with pains unknown to her and then she fainted.

King Sauriyo, who had calmed down, gathered all the dignitaries in the kingdom. He ordered that the riches and the treasures be collected. When everything was ready, he led the convoy and went to the camp of the victorious kings. **(Figure 46)**

Figure 45

Figure 46

In the allied armies, numerous flags and banners indicated the camps of the ministers, of the generals and the troops; the pieces of cloth of different sizes and colors were triumphantly fluttering in the wind.

The old sovereign asked the first soldiers where the kings were. They pointed out to him a red flag far away and he went there. When he arrived, he stopped and was about to bow. The soldiers of that troop came down from their pavilion and said to him: "Oh king, you do not have to bow in front of us; we are only humble warriors born into the station of the people, the kings' servants."

Then the old king said: "Oh warriors of the victorious army, I am the defeated king, I have come to greet your kings. Tell me where they are; show me the way!"

The warriors replied: "Dear king, you will find our sovereigns and masters near the green banner, over there on the horizon."

The old king arrived and prepared to bow. The generals who camped in that place stopped him and pointed to another group.

He wandered in the midst of the innumerable army, consumed by pains. "What a terrible situation I find myself in!" he said to himself.

> Why am I being tromped around if not to have an excuse to make me perish by making me miss the time of the meeting? By submitting myself to my adversaries, I believed I was going to find a little generosity. I was at least hoping they would spare my life! Why are they imposing so much shame and suffering on me? If only I could, before the end of the day, see my two triumphant adversaries, I might find their hearts sympathetic enough to let me live. I am obsessed by this frightful doubt; my chest is violently shaken!

In the meantime, the sun was going down rapidly. Affected by fatigue and pain, the King felt he was going to weaken on the way. He reached a camp that he was assured was that of the kings; it seemed to him it was the last one of the army. He bowed down.

Some chiefs greeted him: "Oh king, why are you doing us this honour? Save it for the sovereigns whose ministers we are!" Seeing that he had no strength left in him, they had him taken to the magnificent platform of the allied kings.

The sight of the powerful triumphant men made King Sauriyo even more worried and he knelt down.

"King, why are you taking this imploring attitude? Your age demands that we treat you as if you were our father; come and join us!"

Those words increased his fear; he dared not to go up to the platform. He remained kneeling on the ground, bowed in front of the sovereigns, putting his hands up to his forehead. The two brothers stood up, climbed down the platform and took his hands into theirs. "No, no," they said. "We could not bear that a king, the same age as our father, honored us so much; it would be contrary to all rules and custom."

These words did not reassure the old man. Seeing that the two sovereigns were taking him away by the hands, his whole body shook and he was convinced that they would have him dead.

> Oh, powerful kings, do not worry, I have no thought in the back of my mind, no bad intentions. I haven't spoken badly about you and did not listen to anyone who might have done that. I have come to surrender. In return I beseech you to let me live. I am handing over to you my kingdom, my riches, everything which can satisfy you.

Vorvong and Saurivong retorted:

> Dear King, we have absolutely no intention of taking your life. We have summoned you in order to know your intentions. We do not want you as a tribute and we do not want any submission of that sort. Your son held out against

> us until death; we want to hear from your mouth if you would be willing to bravely carrying on the fight. Do you want to fight or not? This is what we wish to know.

On hearing this, Sauriyo turned pale with fright; he was close to fainting. He was far from imagining that the two victorious kings were the two sons whose destruction he had ordered ten years before.

"How incomprehensible is the character of these two kings," he thought. "I put myself in their hands; I presented them with my kingdom and my riches and they seem to have the desire to fight! They shame me with their words and after offending me without respect, they are now forcing me to combat them. It means they want to take my life!"

> I would not have the nerve to start fighting against you, oh glorious kings. Restrain your anger, let me live and then I will eternally be your grateful servant.

His sons retorted:

> Since our weapons scare you, do not fight! Send your other two sons against us; we want to have a confrontation with them. But why are you on your own? Why didn't they come with you? Why do you leave them in idleness and apathy? Where are they?"

"Mighty kings, my first two sons have been dead for a long time and the third one succumbed under your weapons. My two elder sons were bad-natured and rebellious to my love. As children they were audacious enough to attempt being violent with the second queen. I had them decapitated."

> Since your two sons were just children, can one possibly believe that they would have dared to act like that? What did you know about their crime - only the accusation of the second queen?
>
> Could it be that since she did not like them, she imagined it? If so, wouldn't you have had any consideration for those two sons who today could defend you against your enemies?
>
> Did your anger blind you to the point of ordering the

> killing of your children without checking if they were indeed criminals? Your behavior was then that of an arrogant, bad and ferocious man who, because he is angry, loses his sense of judgement and reason - a heartless and merciless man.
>
> Today, in front of your confused people, you shamelessly surrender to your enemies, trembling with fear like the worst person among the people. Aren't you embarrassed; have you no regrets, no remorse; don't you think you deserve a fair punishment?
>
> Don't you recognise in us those beings whom you casually condemned to death? We are your two sons.

With this statement, the old king was terrified.

"No," he said to himself, "they are not my sons; they are looking for yet another pretext to condemn me. After having unnecessarily provoked me to fighting, when they heard I had my two sons decapitated, they now pretend to be them. Their aggressive words are announcing, poor creature that I am, that my last hour is approaching!"

> Oh mighty sovereigns, I admit I was wrong in causing my children's death in that manner. I was already old and my mind was weakened. Under the violence of anger prompted by a woman, I gave that order without consideration for my children and my blood.
>
> Pardon me, oh kings! Don't make the situation of a defeated person worse by saying you are the ones whose death I ordered. Be grand and generous; do not increase the burden that the war is putting on my old age and let me continue to live!

Vorvong and Saurivong then clearly understood that their father did not recognise them, that he was close to losing his mind, and so, full of respect, they threw themselves at his feet and said:

> Oh father, we are the two boys whom you expelled from your heart! **(Figure 47)** Be assured that we are those two brothers, your two sons! Have no more doubts, our names are Vorvong and Saurivong. Our mother is Neang Tieya. Queen Montea hated us; one day, she took us in her arms, called for help and accused us. When you heard her, you got blinded by anger and without wanting to hear any further,

Figure 47

you gave the order to have us killed. Our mother, panicking, followed us into the woods, caught up with us, and covered us with caresses. She cried, fell and rolled onto the ground and died of grief before our own eyes. We prayed to the angels to give her back her life and they answered our prayers. Witnessing this manifestation of the power of the heavens, the executioners chose to set us free.

The two princes also spoke about their lives during that long absence, their being separated, Vorvong's misfortune, his shipwreck, his arrival in Canthop Borey and the scene in the room with the paintings.

The old king had no more doubt; he held his sons tightly in his arms and spoke to them softly and tenderly:

> Dear children, let us thank heaven; your destiny prevented you from dying. How happy I am to see you again; you are mighty, handsome, generous, vigorous and full of youth.
>
> My wrongdoing to you was huge. I lost my mind; I was too much in love with a woman. Her words were my law and I did not want to go deeper into the causes of the event. I lost the love I once had for you; not wanting to bring anything into consideration, I gave the order to have you killed.
>
> Thanks to the mercy of the angels and to the virtue of our destiny, you are alive and both of you are kings. I would never have been able to realize that you were at the head of such an army; never would I have thought that you were after my kingdom. My crime is unforgivable. Please think about my old age and put me aside like a savage and an odious man.

The two young kings bowed down at his feet. "What happened to us because of Neang Montea, a consequence of our previous lives, was written in our destiny."

Straightaway the King sent some ambassadors, an escort and some servants to Queen Tieya in order to have her brought to her children.

An order was given to Neang Montea to present herself on foot. Soon she arrived and King Sauriyo said to her angrily:

> Here you are, Montea, deceitful woman who stole my

sons from me. Hear this: With insincere words concealing hate, you enticed my children to your arms; grabbing them, you then called for help misleading everyone, nobody realising what you were preparing. Tell us now the complete truth!

Frightened, Neang Montea bowed down in tears, saying: "Oh King, what you have just stated is nothing but the truth."

Hearing her confession, the old king ordered that she be taken away and immediately drowned in a lake. **(Figure 48)**

The unfortunate Neang Tieya walked in, surrounded by the respectful army. Overwhelmed with joy she recognised her sons and in tears held them tightly against her body. The whole army, moved, witnessed this scene.

> Oh, dear children, I had despaired of seeing you come back once the ten years had passed. I have not had a single good day in my life during your absence.
>
> With an excess of injustice, your father's anger with me has never faded; Neang Montea fostered it by her hatred!
>
> Today, I am seeing you and I am living again! Without your returning I would have died of sorrow and my corpse would have remained abandoned in my miserable hut.

Then King Sauriyo said:

> Oh wife, be generous and forgive my behavior. Yes, my crime is terrible; I am ashamed to talk about it. Montea who caused it is now dead, as well as Vey Vongsa; it is the punishment for the offense. On the contrary, your destiny is a happy one, you are overwhelmed with joy, you are seeing your sons again and they are both kings! Forgive me for the pain I caused you, oh wife who was once so dear to my heart!

"Oh King, I could not have any feeling of hate or vengeance. My sons are here, they have forgotten and I forgive you everything. Go and live happily as you did before!" **(Figure 49)**

Then, the two young kings introduced their wives, the princesses kneeling respectfully behind them, as well as the small child of the King and the Queen.

King Sauriyo and Neang Tieya felt happy and proud when

Figure 48

Figure 49

they saw the admirable young ladies and Vorvong's son. They took him in their arms and covered him with caresses.

Vorvong and Saurivong then prepared the funeral of their brother Vey Vongsa. A superb monument was raised and inside it the young king's body was laid to rest. During one month and a half, day and night, the priests prayed next to the coffin. **(Figure 50)**

Then the ceremony to dispose of the remaining parts of the body took place. An incalculable number of rockets were launched up into the sky and fireworks illuminated the night.

Everything was as splendid as the celestial celebrations. Garlands of flowers adorned the funerary venue, the surrounding of which turned into a huge garden, was full of trees and artificial fruit. Newly opened flowers were graciously floating in the wind. There was fruit at every degree of ripening; one could have believed they were natural, the imitation was so good!

Sauriyo and the young kings, his sons, placed Vey Vongsa's coffin on the pyre. They begged the deceased to grant them his pardon. Then, some real riches were distributed to the poor.

Once this pious duty was accomplished, the raising of the King, the Queen and of their two sons took place solemnly. Then the brothers, wishing to return to their kingdoms, went to the palace to say farewell to their parents **(Figure 51))**

"Oh father, we hope your reign will be successful. Our kingdoms are without kings and the road is long and difficult. We cannot stay any longer in our native country."

The King, feeling that he should not keep them, said: "Oh children, I cannot aspire to the joy of keeping you with me, but you are my only heirs. If you have to leave, at least allow my grandson to stay with me; he will soon be able to reign in my place!"

Figure 50

Figure 51

"Since you wish to keep him, he is yours," Vorvong replied. "We only ask to take the executioners with us, those who saved our lives; we cannot forget their kindness."

"Dear children, I am full of joy to see that you recognise kindness. When you are in your kingdoms, think of us. You are the only comfort of our old age. Forget about my errors and from time to time, keep us happy by visiting us."

Then Neang Tieya spoke:

> My dear children, your departure will weigh heavily on my heart. I can feel my chest tearing up at the thought of this second separation; your departure makes me sad. I am like a woman at the seaside, bathing her child. Suddenly, taken away by the waves, the small baby leaves her arms. She sobs, whines, pulls out her hair, rolls on the beach launching some calls towards the sky - groans and prayers. Her calls are heard and an angel grabs the child and returns him to her. She feels so happy and now she is crying with joy and love.
>
> I am like that mother, dear children. Why are you leaving me again?

The two princes threw themselves at her feet and said: "Oh mother, how could we leave you in pain; every time that you will ask, we promise that we will come and see you."

Vorvong and his fleet headed towards Chay Borey. He met again with his father-in-law, King Sotat, and asked him to take good care of Queen Rot Vodey. Then he went through the air, accompanied by Neang Kessey, to visit King Thornit. He was then the sacred king of that kingdom, surrounded by the joy of the people and the dignitaries. Vorvong wanted to reward the chief of the executioners for his action, so he made him the second king and went back to Chay Borey.

A long time afterwards King Thornit died and a spectacular ceremony took place for his funeral.

Happiness remained with that great family, their kingdoms flourished and they wisely reigned over their populations who were continually happy.

The kings as well as the queens died at a very old age, they were missed by their people and the whole world and they were admitted to heaven.

END

Undated Photo from *Mission Pavie Indo-Chine, 1879-1895, Etudes Diverses, Volume 3*

Exotic Visions of French Indochina

Unknown Temples of Ancient Cambodia.

ISBN: 978-1-934431-90-0

A Romance of Colonial Cambodia.

ISBN 978-1-934431-94-8

Origins of the Cambodian Ballet.

ISBN: 978-1934431-12-2

A Romance of Colonial Cambodia.

ISBN: 978-1-934431-16-0

Exotic Visions of French Indochina

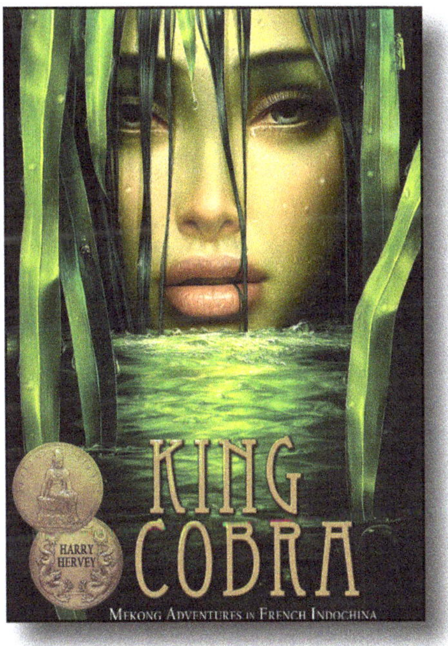

An American in 1920s Indochina.

978-1-934431-82-5

A Sensual Novel of East and West.

978-1-934431-88-7

Fantastic Folktales From Ages Past.

ISBN 978-1-934431-21-4

Analysis of Cambodian Dance

97-8-1934431-29-0

A Rare Artistic Tribute to French Indochina in 1923

French artist André Joyeux published this visually stunning homage to Indochina in memory of his friend, Pierre Rey, who was killed in action during WWI. Joyeux brought each of Rey's 33 French sonnets to life in his series of vibrant watercolors.

This full color, modern edition includes his paintings, the first English translation of the original foreword by Albert Saurraut, former Governor-General of French Indochina, and a biographical profile of both artists in a preface by researcher Joel Montague.

ISBN: 978-1934431917

www.ingramcontent.com/pod-product-compliance
Lightning Source LLC
Chambersburg PA
CBHW042110160726
48295CB00017B/1047

* 9 7 8 1 9 3 4 4 3 1 2 2 1 *